THE FON RETURNS

Fon Tangum

authorHOUSE®

AuthorHouse™ UK
1663 Liberty Drive
Bloomington, IN 47403 USA
www.authorhouse.co.uk
Phone: 0800.197.4150

Published by AuthorHouse 12/08/2015

ISBN: 978-1-5049-9559-7 (sc)
ISBN: 978-1-5049-9560-3 (hc)
ISBN: 978-1-5049-9561-0 (e)

The fon returns is fiction woven on the culture of the graffi people

Among the people of the grass field of Cameroon (commonly referred to as the "graffi"), the belief is that kings – or fons, as the traditional leaders are known there – do not die. When the time comes for one to travel to the land beyond, he is believed to embark on a journey to seek the ancestors of the land, and to return sooner or later, younger, stronger, and wiser, to rule his people. If the fon does not return, the myth holds, the village will cease to exist. What has Ngwokwong done wrong to cause it to move resolutely towards its end? The cry of its people is desperate; their fon still journeys. Will the ancestors of the land let the fon return to his people – or is it the end for this great land?

The answer, it seems, lies beyond the mighty rock – the dwelling of the ancestors of the land – that defiantly stands in the hills of Gam, even to this day.

Chapter 1

The sound of the *ngom* was unmistakable. Its message echoed from the three great hills that almost entirely enclosed the small village of Ngwokwong. Dawn was fast approaching. The glow of the rising sun could be perceived very faintly in the distant horizon behind one of the hills, called "Kob-re-te". The atmosphere was unusually tense. The birds abandoned their early morning singing. The fowls remained silent on the tree branches. The animal world seemed to have melted into thin air. The only usual sound heard was the running of Aghah, the stream that ran the length of the village, and the whispering of the wind as the grasses and trees obstructed its swift and sharp morning motion.

Then the drumming stopped as suddenly as it had started. The village came to life as the people hurried towards its centre. Early risers, like tappers, left their *Raffia* palms unattended and turned their footsteps in the same direction. The strange beats of the ngom had last been heard in Ngwokwong a very long time ago. Only a few elders in the land would remember the exact period. As little groups of women came in sight of the houses that marked out the fon's compound, their voices rose high with exclamations of disbelief and grief. The intermittent

groans and exclamations of the men revealed the gravity of the situation. As the population thickened, the crying and wailing that followed could be heard in the neighbouring villages of Zang, Tugi, and Etwii.

Three men hurried on along a winding path from Zang to Ngwokwong. Although they were not far from the first huts, to them the remaining distance to cover appeared to be unbelievably long. The meandering path they trotted on was quite narrow, and the grass on either side of it overlapped and was covered with dew. Since their departure from Zang, none had spoken. The man leading the way was tall, and his long strides forced those behind to break into a run every now and then. His brows were knit together as he tried to focus his thoughts. This gesture gave him a severe look, which was contrary to his nature. He was not a man of many words. Action to him spoke louder than any number of words put together. His huge *Raffia* bag bounced against his back as he moved along. He recalled many times to himself that a man of his status could not afford to be late, not to mention being absent on such occasions. Fomujang was his name. The birds had still not begun their early morning singing. He hoped sincerely that they remained quiet until he was in the *tawh*[1] hall.

Close behind him was Gyam. He was short and of slim build. His features, with the exception of the deep wrinkles on his face and the white strands of hair on his head, gave him the appearance of a boy. Yet nature had endowed this little man with great talents. He had the sweetness of tongue that made women admire him, effortlessness and ease of expression that attracted young people to him, and guile that turned his enemies into his friends. His face was drawn close, and this was one of the rare moments when one could rightly guess his real age. In reality, he had seen more days

---

[1] *A tawh* is the compound of a fon.

2

than Fomujang. The *Raffia* bag on his back was so small that his cow horn alone occupied the space in it.

At the rear was a tall, athletic young man. His physical features were handsome, and his muscles bulged visibly. The high forehead, deep-set eyes, unusually pointed nose, and the small, tight mouth left no doubt as to whom his father was. Since his tender age, it had become customary for him to accompany Fomujang on his errands, except when his age group was engaged in some previously planned activities. Akatcho was his name. As he moved on behind the two older men, his mind kept darting back to Zang, where he had made a discovery. The drumming had come without warning. He had heard the drumbeat but been unable to make any sense of its message. The beats of the drum had been so strange and unusual. There had been no time for questions. He remembered the worried expression on his father's face as he woke him up. Hurriedly his father had whispered with Awah, their host, before their hasty departure.

Akatcho hated being in the dark. As they drew nearer to Ngwokwong, the wailing that reached them confirmed his suspicions that something awful had happened. Several thoughts crossed his mind, but none stood out or made any sense. As he made up his mind to ask, Gyam groaned with pain, throwing away the almost completely burnt bundle of wood he held in his right hand.

"*Ndonn*! This ill-fated fire almost ate up my fingers," he hissed.

Shaking his head, he remarked, "So the day has broken. It is a wonder that no bird is singing." He rubbed his chin with his palm, in thought. "Good things don't stay long," he mumbled.

Fomujang was aware that once Gyam began talking, their pace was going to slow down. He half swung round.

"Gyam, I believe you realise the risk we are running by moving at a snail's pace." His right index finger whipped the air, pointing for emphasis. The two men behind hurriedly caught up with him.

"Eh, Fomujang, I prefer being late to being absent."

Gyam folded himself together and brushed his left ear with his right palm, as if denying an accusation thrown on him.

"Looking back at what Wunde had to put up with for not attending Ngwana's funeral, I don't think there is any man in Ngwokwong who will dare to cross a river without a bridge," he added.

Wunde had been a hunter of great repute among all the neighboring villages of Ngwokwong and had been held in very high esteem by all. But when Ngwana, a young herder from Tugi village had accidentally died while attempting to save his goat that had been caught in one of Wunde's ingenious traps, many were the people who had cried out loud for the latter to stop his hunting activity. Wunde had been so crossed by the general furore, that he had refused to attend Ngwana's funeral. The elders of Ngwokwong had believed that Ngwana had met his death accidentally by falling into a pit that Wunde had made close to his trap to ensure larger animals did not escape. However, Wunde's behaviour had provoked their wrath and by way of punishment the former had been banned from any hunting activity for a full year. Hunting had been Wunde's means of livelihood all his adult life. The punishment had been too much for him to bear and he had fled from the village and had never been heard of again. The story is still told in Ngwokwong to this day.

"Ah, good memory! You may also know that this is a special case where lateness could have the same consequence as absence," Fomujang added without looking backwards. He was very conscious of the fact that a man of his position was not supposed to be out of Ngwokwong during certain happenings – especially if such an occurrence was predictable. His strides increased, and he quickly outdistanced the others.

The young man did not mind keeping to Gyam's pace. He wanted the details before they reached the village. He moved closer to Gyam.

"Wasn't the day before yesterday the Tang market day?" he asked, trying to bring the other into conversation. Gyam raised his head and noted that the distance between him and Fomujang had increased. He shrugged wearily. He was not the type to remain silent for very long. He could eat and talk at the same time without choking. The only time his presence could not be felt was when he slept. As he cleared his throat, he stumbled over a stump in the middle of the path that had been hidden from sight by overlapping grass. He cursed so bitterly and threw such a threatening glance at the stump that Akatcho burst out with laughter.

"You would not laugh if this helpless devil tore off your flesh. On Tang it caught my right toe, and today it decided to take on the left. I will see what it will do next time, given that I don't have a third leg."

Akatcho respected the silence that followed. Gyam's pain had to subside before he asked any further questions. They were within reach of the first houses, and the noise from the village was escalating. Fomujang had disappeared behind the huts, evidently looking for the shortest path to the tawh. It was not the fear of arriving late that urged Gyam to pull Akatcho to his side but the desire to talk.

"Come closer, my child," he said. "I know you are itching with the desire to know what is happening."

"That's true," the young man whispered.

"Well, on Tang, our fon's[2] illness appeared to give way. On your father's invitation, I followed him to Zang, where we met you. I thought we would be there for at least three days. In fact, I meant to show those feeble sons of Zang that, we, the Ngwokwong men, can treat palm wine just as we do our special *Raffia* wine." He passed his tongue over his lips and whipped the air with his right index finger. That indicated an occasion narrowly missed.

The crying that reached them now was deafening. Akatcho had no more doubts as to the cause.

"It is the fon." His eyes asked, but his mouth simply said it. Gyam nodded slowly, and in mournful silence they moved into the swarming tawh.

---

[2] In the tradition and culture of the people of the grass field of Cameroon, the fon is the ruler of a village. *A* man who gets that status is hardly *ever* called by his name. He is *called* either "the fon" or "the father" of his people.

Chapter 2

The tawh yard presented a pathetic sight. Women crawled all over, smacking their thighs and crying so distressingly that there wasn't the least doubt how much love and respect they had for the departed. Even the very young children, who hardly understood what was happening, rolled in the dust, and tears ran down their cheeks. A few men sat on the huge logs of wood lined up along the sides of the huts. Many of them supported their heads with their palms and gazed into space.

Gyam and Akatcho made their way with difficulty past the mourning women. Darkness had completely given way to daylight, and the people could now begin to make out clearly who their neighbours were. As they neared the entrance to the reception hall, Akatcho spotted his friend Sango in conversation with his mother.  The woman sprawled in the dust, apparently worn out with crying. While Gyam walked into the hall, Akatcho directed his steps toward his friend. "Sango," he called.

The young man straightened and turned around. As he looked at his friend, he inhaled deeply. "Akatcho," he said, shaking his head slowly and sorrowfully, "you came alone? Where is baba Fomujang?"

Akatcho stretched his lips in the direction of the hall.

"Let's go in too," Sango suggested.

The hall was sufficiently spacious. The men, young and old, sat on stools along the internal walls. There was absolute silence, and sorrow could be read on all the men's faces. Some of them let their tears flow freely. Even the various skulls that were suspended from long, thin strings on the walls did not rattle in the early morning breeze. The two young men moved across the room to where most of their mates sat. Finding no free stools, they threw themselves on the bare floor and waited in respectful silence. Their eyes wandered round the room; they were not certain what next would happen.

Across the room, opposite to where they sat, was a vacant stool. Its round-shaped top was covered with a white fur of sheepskin. The stool was painted black, and the many curious designs on its sides revealed the hardness and thickness of the wood from which it was made. At the foot of the chair was a huge cow horn, blackened with age and use. It had served four generations of fons. Quite close to it was a round-bottomed calabash with a small hole on its neck. On the wall behind the stool was a short, stout stick that obviously had served as a third leg for the fon.

On either side of the stool sat two elderly men, each holding his traditional fibrous black cap in his hands. The taller man sitting to the right was Forkon. He was of slight build, and his small, regular face, with its deep wrinkles, showed him as a man of advanced age. His grey hair was sparse, and his head and shoulders hung a little forward. He sat still, looking intently at the floor. He had turned towards the wall behind him to adjust an old wooden gun leaning on the wall there. To the left side of the stool sat Abanda. He was of solid stature and a little shorter than Forkon. His hair was a mixture of black and white. His face was broad and lean. He had a much shorter beard than Forkon's. He stared contemplatively at the stool. These two men were the closest advisers to the fon. With the latter on his way onto the land of the ancestors, they knew that the responsibility of ensuring a smooth transition rested fully on their shoulders.

The happenings of the previous night had been as dramatic as they were inexplicably disturbing. The fon had been very ill for a couple of weeks, and the elders of the land had prepared themselves for the worst. It had happened a few minutes before midnight. Forkon and Abanda had intermittently taken position by his bedside since the illness had worsened a fortnight back. When the fon had stepped onto the path leading to the ancestors of the land that late evening, it had been Forkon's turn by his bedside. The fon had made frantic efforts to whisper something into Forkon's ear but only mumbled inaudible and inarticulate sounds that did not quite make sense to the latter. As the fon became restless and very agitated, Forkon had stepped to the door to call Ba-yoh, the fon's eldest son.

As both returned to the room, the fon was very still, and they both knew that the journey to the ancestral fold had begun. Forkon had turned towards Ba-yoh and placed his right hand on his shoulder. "Stay here, my son, and I will go and summon the elders," he had whispered.

Ba-yoh was a middle-aged man who, despite his rank, was very reserved and hardly showed any emotion. He had just stood there, staring at the lifeless body on the bed, and did not react to Forkon's words. Forkon had hurried out of the room and had quickly sent two men to summon the elders of the land. Within a short time, they had gathered at the fon's reception hall and were whispering among themselves. Quick decisions and plans were agreed on, and each elder went off to accomplish his task. One of the elders of the land, Fomujang, had been absent. Forkon had been surprised that no one knew where Fomujang had gone. As each of the elders left to accomplish his task, Forkon and Abanda had turned towards the fon's inner chamber. As the recollection came vividly into Forkon's mind, he shivered visibly on his stool. He drew in a very deep breath as he tried hard to discard the recollection and the unanswered questions that had been jamming his mind. As the two men had entered the room and their eyes had accustomed to the darkness, they had seen Ba-yoh's body slumped across the lifeless one of the fon. These two experienced elders did not have to stare long to understand that Ba-yoh had embarked on the same journey as his father. This type of event had never happened before in Ngwokwong or any other land known to the elders of the land. They both had remembered then the curse of Djalo some years back, as had been narrated to them under oath by their fon. It had been a well-kept secret, and it had gradually receded to the back of their minds over the years.

Suddenly a cock's crow sounded somewhere behind the hall. The older men began to straighten their bodies on their stools, turning their heads in the direction of the empty stool. The younger men swung their heads from left to right, wondering what was going to happen next. Slowly, Forkon raised his head and drew in a deep breath. Sighing deeply, he rose with visible effort from his stool. His eyes widened and reddened. He joined his hands in front of him, and his lips parted.

"Ngwokwong! Oh, Ngwokwong!" His voice was sonorous. "What a loss. What a mighty loss for our people." He paused to catch his breath after the pressure he had endured since the late hours of last night.

"All the same, it has happened, and like the great sons of Ngwokwong that we are, we must bear the great loss with courage. We must prove first to ourselves and then to our neighbours that we are the true children of our departed father, by carrying on the proceedings, as befits our tradition. We must at the same time proceed in a way as to accommodate the actions imposed by the extraordinary demise of Ba-yoh, our father's eldest son."

Some women and children stood by the door. When they saw him turn and clasp the old gun behind him, they scrambled to the farthest ends of the yard, their hands pressing against their ears. Forkon marched like a warrior, the gun across his shoulder, to the door. Back in the hall, the older men were busy loading their wooden guns with gunpowder. The women and children were clinging tightly to each other. Forkon raised the gun onto his right shoulder. He stood astride the threshold, the gun pointing at the mighty rock at the summit of the tallest of the hills. The giant rock seemed to emerge from the depths of the hill and rise high into the sky. It had stood there over the ages and still stands majestically in Ngwokwong to this day. It is called Kob Azah, meaning "the rock of Azah". It is considered the dwelling place of the ancestors of the land.

"It is time Ngwokwong announced the disappearance of her great son." Forkon's voice was loud and steady. His hands trembled slightly, and the gun suspended in mid-air for a brief moment. Then without warning, it roared thunderously. The ground trembled, and for a long moment only the echo from the hills resounded in the air. As Forkon walked back to his seat, the men left their stools and moved onto the almost-deserted yard. Most of the women and children had hurried away into the huts. For a long while, the air was filled with deafening noise as the guns reported the grief of the Ngwokwong people to the outside world.

When all the men had returned to their seats, Forkon raised his voice for all to hear. "I will need four or five others with me to prepare him that was not given the opportunity to guide his people – as his father before him had done – for the long journey he has embarked on."

Grey-haired men, all eager to pay their last physical respects and duty to the departed, instantly joined him. They disappeared into the little room in which the body of Ba-yoh lay.

Abanda rose to his feet. The attention of all who remained in the hall focussed on him. His eyes seemed to pierce the air in front of him as they made a round of the room. Traces of tears showed on his cheeks. He blew his nostrils noisily and then rubbed his palms together. He quickly arrested the gesture, and his lips twisted, expressing real pain. His palms had developed blisters from the hard work done that early morning as the elders of the land had prepared and sent off the remains of the fon on his journey to the land beyond and prayed ardently for his quick return. According to the tradition of the land, a fon did not die. When the time for one came to join the ancestors of the land, only a selected few elders were involved with the preparation and burial. Neither the grave nor the moment of burial of a fon was known; he was believed to have disappeared and embarked on a journey to seek the ancestors of the land. But he would return someday, younger, stronger, and wiser, to rule his people. If the ancestors of the land were happy with the fon during his reign and with the village as a whole, then the fon would return sooner than later to continue leading his people.

"The Gods have made their decision," Abanda told them. "Bitter though it is, we must accept it so. If you go to a battle and lose your right hand, you will need time to train the left to be as effective as the right. Yes, time and pain will be involved." His voice rose and fell at regular intervals. "Our father has embarked on his journey. Ba-yoh, our father's son cannot make the same journey as his father. Let the young men who had looked on him as a brother and potential future father of this land follow me. We must prepare for him a resting place worthy of his rank and love."

His eyes settled on the young men, and Akatcho had the feeling that he was looking straight at him. He jumped to his feet, and other young men instantly joined him. At the threshold, Abanda paused and looked back into the room.

"Fomujang," he called.

"Ah-haa," Fomujang answered and walked towards the door.

"I think you should get two or three boys with you to the hill and choose two sheep. That would not be too small, I hope?"

"Yaah. I think two will be enough for today. That should keep our visitors' mouths occupied for a while."

Abanda nodded and led the boys out. Fomujang returned to the room and, noticing that Sango was rushing out after the others, called out, "Ah! Sango, you come with me to the hill. Call along two others."

At the corner where he sat, Gyam gritted his teeth and folded himself together, apparently unhappy with his neighbours, who ignored his repeated attempts to bring them into some conversation. Outside, the crowd was growing rapidly. The Etwii people, being the nearest neighbours, were the first to arrive. The men carried their wooden guns on their shoulders. The women followed the men in mournful silence, their hands folded across their breasts as if reacting to the morning cold. As they came onto the scene, they threw themselves on the ground and burst into tears. The younger men preferred sitting on the logs outside, while the older ones walked directly into the tawh hall.

Behind the large hut, the young men worked arduously. Akatcho was down in the almost-finished grave. The hoe he used crashed every now and then against stones buried in the bowels of the earth. He had hardly spoken to those above, except when he asked for a spade to replace the hoe he had been using. He filled basket after basket with soil and raised them to those above. The mound of soil around the grave was quite significant. After he sent up the last basket, he was himself pulled up and out.

Of all the boys, only Mbanwi had done nothing. He was not the type from whom much physical work could be expected. He looked with undisguised admiration at the muscular form of Akatcho.

"You have done half the digging alone." His voice was thin and high-pitched. Akatcho hardly heard him. He was busy wiping the perspiration from his body. Mbanwi was of very slender build, and the only thing he excelled in was talking.

"I think you will—" he was saying, when Gyam's voice called from the corner of the house. He had apparently not found people who paid attention to his endless attempts at calling attention to himself.

"Are you through?" Gyam asked

Mbanwi rubbed his stomach with both palms as he answered;

"Everything has been perfectly done,". He sounded as if he had done the job all by himself.

"Ah!" Gyam was shaking his head in appreciation.

"The earlier you finish, the better, because, as I can see, people's worms have finished all what was in their stomachs and now are tearing at their intestines." He drew nearer to look at the grave.

"You have done well, my children. We can go now and see what next should be done. I have always said that you boys have no rivals. Those young men from Zang only know how to woo girls – not to mention those of Etwii." Gyam stopped talking and quickly looked around. Abanda was not there. He felt more at ease.

Akatcho tried to divert the conversation. "Have the sheep been brought from the hill?"

"Ah, you again. Do you think the hill is where people go to without returning?" Mbanwi was annoyed. Gyam had just touched one of his favourite topics.

"Have they come or not?" Akatcho's voice was hard and snappy.

"I do not know why they have not come back yet." Gyam was aware of Akatcho's hot temper. "We expected them to be back by the time you had done half your job. However, I think—"

"I will go and check." Akatcho said briskly and moved past them. The other boys followed him to the front of the house. Mbanwi remained at the rear, hoping to provoke Gyam into their usual vulgar conversation. How people could create fun at such grave moments was beyond Akatcho. He moved carefully among the women in the yard. The ear-splitting wailing had reduced to sobs and moans. The women were completely covered with dust, and most of them blew their nostrils noisily to get rid of the layer of dust that had found its way in.

Akatcho raised his left hand to his face, shading his eyes from the rising intensity of the sun. His eyes swept across the kob-re-te hill. As he was turning his head, he noticed a movement at the extreme end of the hill, from where one could stand and look down onto the elliptically shaped village of Etwii. He looked intently and noticed a human figure, closely followed by a huge cow. Behind came two more figures and a third one that seemed to be pulling along two white sheep.

He turned and moved into the hall. The room was filled with noises. He made his way towards Gyam, who had returned to his seat. Awah sat next to him. It was in his house at Zang that the message of the ngom had reached Fomujang and Gyam. Akatcho stood before them and was not immediately noticed.

"*Miyaka babaa,*" Akatcho greeted Awah. He respected this old but strong-looking man. "Did Angye not come with you?".

Awah looked up. "Ah! You are well, my son? Eh, he will be coming later with some palm wine. You see, I could not stay back to look for wine. When you left, I did not stay long before following."

Akatcho nodded to show he followed what Awah was saying. Then he turned and rushed out.

"May our great gods bless you." Gyam chuckled. "You cannot imagine the hell I have gone through. After promising my worms that I was going to drown them in palm wine, what else could they do other than tear apart my intestines on my failure to satisfy them? Right now, they are doing their worst." As he spoke, he threw anxious looks outside to see whether Angye, Awah's son, was coming. Awah looked worried. He looked entreatingly at his friend.

"Please, Gyam," he pleaded, "you cannot afford to ignore the reason for this gathering. You are aware of how you Ngwokwong people misinterpret words." Gyam folded himself up and hoped someone would think how to solve his problem.

Chapter 3

Akatcho made his way along the ridges to the foot of the hill. The farmlands flourished with maize, bean, and groundnut crops. When he came within hearing distance, he looked uphill, and saw Sango and the other two boys desperately attempting to urge a cow to move. While Sango pulled hard at the rope that was tied around the cow's neck, the boys kept hitting the ground with their heels and uttering noises in imitation of *ganakos or* shepherds. The cow just stood its ground, apparently determined not to budge. The boys stood looking at the animal helplessly, not knowing what else to do.

Akatcho noiselessly hurried to the scene. "Heh, Sango! Is that cow refusing to move?" he asked with excitement in his voice. His muscles twitched, and his imagination swirled with ideas to resolve the situation.

The other two boys stared past Sango. The latter swung round and heaved a sigh of relief as he saw his friend. He stood with his back turned to the cow. "*Ouf!* What a relief. I was just thinking of sending Mbah to come and call for you."

The mere sight of Akatcho had sent fear and worrying out of the young men. Fomujang was tying up the sheep to a nearby shrub and noted with inward pride the comfort and assurance that his son's presence brought.

"How come you are bringing a cow?" Akatcho asked, coming up to Sango's side.

"We met Lamu leading his cows to the valley," Sango explained. "When he learnt what had happened, he sat down shaking his head in disbelief.

He went amongst his cows and chose this one to help Ngwokwong feed her expected visitors."

Akatcho sized up the cow. "Despite their exclusive way of life, these *Bororo* people are very caring. I will get a big stick to make it move." He turned and ran towards a nearby tree. The sun had been steadily rising in the sky. The heat was increasing too. Large drops of sweat showed on the boys' faces. As they waited for Akatcho's return, their thoughts trailed back to the fon's compound. They strained their ears to catch any noises that could give an indication of what was taking place.

Fomujang had found a comfortable spot to sit down and was trying to imagine Ngwokwong without the departed. Unwanted thoughts invaded his mind. That the fon had embarked on his last errand was predictable, given his ailment and age. But why would he take along his first son? Or did the gods want to express their anger for some wrongdoing? He was slowly shaking his head with sadness when, by a stroke of luck, his eyes caught a quick movement.

"Look out!" his voice rang through the air. "The cow has broken loose."

Swiftly, Sango spun round and dived sideways, just in time to avoid the cow's thrusting long horns. The other two boys had slackened their hold on the ropes that were tied to the cow's hind legs. The sudden forward rush of the cow threw them to the ground. They scrambled to their feet and began pulling with all their might. Sango tried to rise, but the pain in his left arm was excruciating. He struggled to a sitting position and only moaned with agony.

"Keep pulling with all your might."

The cow had been slowly gaining on the boys and had lowered its horns, preparing to bury them deep in its victim's bowels. However, the excited voice of Akatcho invigorated the boys, and the cow's progress was checked. Akatcho held a huge stick in his hand. Realising the uselessness of it at the moment, he threw it aside and rushed to Sango's side. He wanted to help his friend out of the way, but at that very moment, he saw that the cow was beginning to move again. He abandoned his first idea and picked up the rope Sango had been holding. He ran round the cow, holding firmly to the rope and jumping over the ropes the other boys were pulling. When he had made a complete circle and a half, he saw that the rope had reduced considerably in length. He pulled out so abruptly and mightily that the cow had no alternative but to come down in one great heap. All three boys rushed to it and quickly bound its hind legs firmly as the animal struggled to rise.

Fomujang drew nearer to Sango. He had started out to help the two boys pull back at the cow. However, as soon as his son had come up, taking full command of the situation, he had diverted his attention to the injured young man.

"Are you badly hurt?" he asked.

"I fell on my left arm, and I fear my wrist is broken," Sango mumbled with pain.

Fomujang held the arm and gently pulled at it. "This is to readjust any bones that may have missed their place," he explained soothingly. Akatcho came to his friend's side.

"Are you hurt?"

"My wrist aches awfully. Were it not for Father, I think I should be talking from the other world. How do we carry that mass down?"

"The rest of us will look into that. I think you should go to Mother now, so she may treat your hand." Akatcho turned towards the others. "Would you mind accompanying him, Mbah?"

One of the boys supported Sango to his feet, and they began descending homewards.

"Would you lead the sheep to the tawh, Father, while I rush down and seek help from Abanda to move the cow?"

Fomujang grunted his assent with a faint smile.

Akatcho turned to the other young man, Forwah. "You want to stay and wait for me? The cow cannot do any harm now."

The young man nodded but threw a suspicious look at the animal. "I will feel more at ease sitting under the tree over there, just in case its ropes come off."

"You are right," Akatcho agreed, sizing up the eucalyptus tree Forwah was pointing at. "I know you can go up the tree faster than a monkey."

He turned and began jumping across the ridges on his way downhill. Fomujang followed him with his eyes until he had gone out of sight. Then he turned and moved with proud steps towards the sheep.

As he drew nearer to the tawh, Akatcho noticed that there was silence. He imagined what was taking place in the compound. He reached the yard and moved silently to the back of the hall. The crowd around the grave was thick. Those who stood at its edge were looking down sadly at its content. Among the people were the fons of the neighbouring villages – a very unusual sight. According to the tradition of Ngwokwong and all its neighbouring villages, a fon was immortal but could disappear into the land beyond. By virtue of his immortality, he did not see a corpse or attend a burial.

What was happening in Ngwokwong was unprecedented in this and the neighbouring villages. Fear and uncertainty could be felt among the elders of the land and beyond. When a fon disappeared and his heir followed immediately, whatever the circumstances, it was enough to throw any village into a turmoil. And when, in addition to this inexplicable happening, another prince had been gone beyond the boundaries of the land to some unknown destination for many years, many are those who began to convince themselves that Ngwokwong had one way or another provoked the wrath of the gods and could cease to exist. The situation of Ngwokwong was desperately extraordinary, and only the special intervention of the fons could appease the ancestors and gods of the land.

At the edge where he stood, Forkon waited for total silence. Some of the women still sobbed and blew their noses. Slowly, very slowly, Forkon raised his head from what he had been looking at. He swallowed hard and felt pains in his throat.

"Ngwokwong Oh, Ngwokwong!" He paused as if to regain his breath. "Our forefathers used to say that what makes a man a leader of his people is his head, because it carries the eyes that show him the way, ears that hear the cry of his people, and a mouth that spreads wisdom. Today we are beginning to feel the absence of our head."

He stopped and looked into the grave. He spread his ten fingers, pointing at its content. "The head lying here never had the opportunity to lead its people. The father of Ngwokwong has gone on a long journey. He had led us onto a clean and sure path of peace and happiness. He could have returned as he who lies here below. But that will never happen, as we now know".

Forkon's words only provoked more shedding of tears.

"Before we cover him up with soil that will protect him from the heat of the sun, the cold of the rains, and the violence of the wind, I will repeat the very last words of our departed father to you, his children."

Forkon shifted his ground a little and looked round, his eyes burning. Those who stood close to him heard the gnashing of his teeth. It was usual with him when he had something very important to say. He stretched out his hands with his palms upturned.

"Live like one man, and keep to the path of our ancestors. Let our laws and tradition be the solution to any challenges that you may confront. Look after your mouths, as mothers look after their babies, for it is the mouth that provokes trouble and does not assist in the physical confrontation that may result. Chew your words until they are as smooth as your *foofoo* before letting them out."

The men threw anxious glances at the women who stood at a respectable distance away, as if the last words were particularly meant for them. Forkon raised his eyes, and they met those of the young fon of Etwii. He bowed significantly. The fon was dressed in a traditional robe that carried various designs. He held a short staff in his left hand. Despite his young age, he had developed a huge personality associated with his rank. All eyes settled on him. He drew a step forward and slowly looked round at the thick crowd. Then, for a brief moment, his mind went back to that horrible day, many years back in his tawh.

He had been very young then, his chin still smooth. He had carried a calabash of *Raffia* wine from the inner chamber to the fon, his father, as the latter relaxed on his traditional sofa, enjoying the early morning sun. The old man had drunk a horn full of *Raffia* wine and had expressed his satisfaction in the same words the young man had heard on several other occasions: "I bless the gods for guiding my decision to give my daughter to Ba-yoh of Ngwokwong in marriage. Just see how he takes care of me. I hope you, too, will be great friends when you grow up, my son."

That relaxed atmosphere had suddenly grown tense as Djalo, the *Bororo* man who lived at the summit of the hill called kob-re-mbu and overlooking the fon's farmland, had rushed into the tawh yard, panting and sweating profusely.

"He has killed all my cows," he had stammered. "Ba-yoh has killed all that I have!" Then Djalo had thrown himself at the fon's feet, wailing.

"What happened?" the fon had asked.

"*Wallai*! Ba-yoh dug a huge pit at the edge of his farm, and fourty of my fourty eight cows have fallen into it and died," Djalo explained between sobs. He was very fluent with the local language.

"That land is mine. I gave it to Ba-yoh to grow food and feed my daughter, his wife." Why did you not direct your cows away from the farm?" the fon had asked.

"Wallai! How was I to know that farming was going on in that bush? You know yourself that for many moons no one farmed there, and I took my cows there often for grazing."

Djalo had burst out wailing again. "Instead of killing my cows, Ba-yoh should have called for me to settle the matter. How can I live without my cows? How can I provide for my family?"

"You should return to your compound. I will discuss the matter with the Fon of Ngwokwong," the fon had advised.

Djalo had stopped crying and had staggered to his feet. "I will take my leave now." He had suddenly become calm. "I will go home. I do not want to feel pain any more. But I will say this: Ba-yoh will never live to become the fon of his people!"

Djalo had turned and dragged himself away.

The following morning, his body had been found dangling from a rope around his neck, tied to a branch of the tallest tree at the centre of the farm where his cows had met their fate.

With a deep sigh, the young Fon directed his eyes into the grave, his right fingers spread and pointing at its contents.

"And there, oh Ngwokwong, lies the embodiment of tradition, truth, and wisdom. What can a man do against the wish of the gods?" He slowly looked round as if expecting an answer. He was convinced within himself that the gods had had no hand in Ba-yoh's fate. Some truths were better withheld for the sake of peace.

"Nothing. Yes, nothing," he said, shaking his head sadly.

"My dear children of Ngwokwong," he called in a raised voice so all could hear his words, "you know as well as I do that only one path leads to victory. If you believed in him that fathered the deceased and his love for peace – among us, and between us and others whom the Gods have brought to live among us – then his spirit will continue to direct your steps towards happiness, freedom, and unity." He waited a moment for his words to sink in.

"Ngwokwong," he went on, "you had one of the rare heads and fathers of our time. I myself came to him for advice, for after everything, he was my father too. If you keep to his footprints, then happiness and peace will be your portion. May our ancestors accept him in their midst."

He stepped backwards to his former position. The Fon of Zang moved forward. He carried an air of responsibility and authority about him. He coughed to clear his throat. His small nostrils widened as he opened his mouth to speak. "Oh! Children of Azah." His voice was well modulated.

He looked expectantly around. Indeed, something did happen. Until then, some people had still felt they were living a dream. But when the name of the deceased was pronounced, they came back to reality and began to sob quietly.

"Yes, Azah has preceded us. We all shall in turn follow this very path."

Some of the people became a little frightened when he put their fears into words. Raising his staff, the fon continued, "If you plant yams today and harvest them tomorrow, without planting those for the days ahead, then you invite trouble."

He shook his staff as he explained. "Azah has fed you, his children, with wisdom. If you fail to live by it, you lose your peace and happiness. If you fail to pass his wisdom unto your children, our descendants, you lose your ancient glory and dignity."

Turning his face into the grave, he spoke to the dead. "Oh, Azah! Wherever you are, don't forget your children still thirst for your wisdom and light. What has happened is only the decision of the gods. And no one shall question that. You were never to return as he who lies here below. But you shall return. Your people need you. We need you. I, fon Teghenicha, implore our ancestors to forgive the people of Ngwokwong any wrong that may have been done knowingly or not. May your return be sooner rather than later."

The Fon of Tugi immediately stepped forward, like one who had long been holding his patience. He was tall and of slight build. His brows were always knit, and his lips seemed to push forward. His jaw bones stood out prominently. The curiously carved stick in his right hand served as a third leg for this stooping old man. He was known for making long speeches. There was a general movement as the people adjusted themselves, evidently expecting the fon to keep them standing for long.

The Fon raised his eyes towards the mighty rock. All present turned their eyes in the same direction, with visible awe on their faces. Slowly his right hand rose above his head. His left hand firmly gripped his staff to support his frame.

"Azah has done everything." The right hand speedily came down for emphasis. "Yet, sons and daughters of Azah, everything still remains to be done. I, fon Mbakwa of Tugi ask our ancestors who reside in the mighty kob Azah to look down with favour on our people." And to the consternation of all, he stepped back to his original position and calmly placed his right palm on his chest.

Forkon quickly recovered. He cleared his throat. "The time has come for us to give our would-have-been father the last farewell," he said. He nodded to the Fon of Zang. The fon picked up a handful of soil, which he dropped into the grave, after murmuring a few words of farewell. The other two fons followed his example. Then Forkon led the fons back to the hall, amidst silence as the people stepped out of the way and stooped in respect of the custodians of the laws and traditions of their lands.

Then all eyes settled on Abanda, the late fon's other close adviser. The latter, a bit weary from the work done during the previous night with the revered and secret burial of their departed head, waited until the fons had disappeared into the hall. "Ngwokwong, it is your turn," he announced.

The population moved forward, and before long, the mat in which the dead man was wrapped had disappeared from sight.

Chapter 4

When the grave had regained the ground level, the people began dragging their legs back to the tawh yard. There was still silence as the men took their places in the hall again. Abanda was whispering to Mimba when Akatcho came up to him. Akatcho stood respectfully waiting for Abanda to finish what he was saying to the other.

Abanda's penetrating eyes did not miss the suppressed excitement of the young man. "Yes, my son. Is anything the matter?"

"Yes. The cow was too stubborn to be pulled up to here. So we—"

"Did you say a *cow*?" Abanda showed his surprise.

"It was given by Lamu when he learned what has happened. It is lying at the foot of the hill, where we tied it in case it gets loose."

Abanda rubbed his beard thoughtfully.

Mimba stood by his side, waiting to resume his conversation. He was a strong middle-aged man. Around his waist was tied a knife after the *Bororo* fashion. He had won a reputation in Ngwokwong as the man with the sharpest knife.

Abanda turned toward him. "We were just talking about the sheep. H'mmm, now it looks as if you will also take care of a cow. You know you are the best man for that."

Mimba smiled. He liked compliments.

"The only problem will be that of conveying the meat downhill." Mimba gave the impression that his own part of the job could be considered done.

"Get as many girls as you need to help carry the meat down here."

Mimba nodded and caught Akatcho's hand. They rushed out.

By then, most of the men were seated in the tawh hall. Forkon rose from his seat and joined his fingertips. He bowed deeply, facing the fons as they sat to one side of the empty stool.

"Mbeeeh." Forkon greeted the fons in the traditional manner. Then he turned towards the others in the room. "Beloved sons of Ngwokwong, our father has embarked on his journey. Were he here now, he would not be happy to see us just seated and waiting for the unknown. We must do something worthy of our great head."

There was a pause.

"It is true, oh my brothers, that we shall all follow this singular path. But before any of us is forced into it, let each man do his utmost for the sake of our land and posterity."

He raised his voice, cheering up slightly. "Of course, nothing can be done with empty stomachs. Our forefathers used to say that a bird with an empty stomach can never build its nest to completion, even if it puts in all its energy. Our throats are dry as well. Before we put our heads and hands together and do that which we must do to keep to the path of our ancestors, we must first obey the fundamental law of nature."

He threw a meaningful look at Abanda. The latter took two boys with him into an inner room, which was filled with the smell of *Raffia* wine. Several jugs and calabashes were neatly arranged at one corner of the room. At the corner opposite to the jugs was a huge pot, blackened with age and use. It was built of clay, round bottomed and broadened out at the middle. It curved inwards at the neck and stood about sixty centimetres above the floor.

Abanda called to the young men near him, "Nyanga, come and carry this pot to the hall. Ngoh, you carry that jug over there. I will get the smaller calabashes."

Ngoh shook his head when he saw the jug pointed out to him. He thought he would not be able to lift it from the ground.

"Call somebody to help you," Abanda said and turned to take down the calabashes hanging from the wall. As he turned to move back into the room, he saw Akatcho lifting the jug onto his shoulder while Ngoh stood by with wide-open eyes. He smiled with admiration for this young man, in whom he already saw his successor.

They moved into the hall and emptied the contents of the jugs into the huge pot. The two boys each held a calabash, and at a sign from Forkon, they filled them. They were going to start distributing, when a voice spoke. Very few people heard or saw the speaker, as most of the men were busy blowing the dust from their horns, their minds focused on the pot of wine. When the voice spoke again, all heads turned towards the Fon of Tugi. He cleared his throat and stared round the room.

"Mbeeeh," came the response from the people.

Sitting straight on his stool, his legs spread wide apart and palms closed on each knee, the fon swept his stern look through the room.

"My beloved children of Ngwokwong," he began, "the disappearance of our great brother and father has hit us all right into our bones. Our fathers of long ago said that when a man loses his nose, his two eyes shed tears."

He watched the faces in the room. Most of the older men understood him, and they rubbed their white beards with guilt. Some even put down their horns. Gyam understood the saying of the ancestors. He threw a desperate stare at the pot of wine and then at the fon.

"I see many of you, particularly our children who are still growing into manhood, don't understand the saying of our forefathers. Let me tell you what it means."

He paused and pointed his forefinger around at the men. "You, the men, make one eye." Then, tracing a circular path in the air, his finger pointing outside, he continued, "They, too, make an eye. The departed is the nose. If you are thirsty and hungry, know also that your women are not made of stone but of flesh and blood. My nostrils inform me that the women are doing the cooking now. I am certain they have us in mind as they do so. I will therefore implore you to send a jug or at least a calabash of wine to them."

He added with a wan smile, which loosened the folds of his face, "Don't forget that some of your wives are with babies, and they have to fill their breasts." He tapped his right foot slowly on the ground and looked at his two colleagues, who nodded in approval.

Forkon sat motionlessly. As soon as he had heard the fon's proverb, his mind had started racing. He realised his mistake but decided to put up some defence. He stood up when the fon had ended his reproach.

"Mbeeeh," he began, "we thank you for your wisdom. We cannot forget our women who are sharing in our grief, except we decided to become the cock which cares for the hen only when it wants to meet it the way we meet our wives in our huts."

Forkon waited for the noise that rose to die down. He continued, "We know our women well. They lack the resistance of the Zang women, who can drink palm wine and yet keep clear heads. If we haven't sent a jug to our wives and children, it is for fear that they may add excess salt or pepper in the food they are preparing."

The guilt on most of the faces in the room began to disappear. Forkon was a clever speaker. He knew that if he did not tackle the fon's accusation carefully, Ngwokwong was going to be mocked for a long time.

"However," Forkon kept on, "what our father said was very right, for our wives may fail to understand our reason for depriving them of wine at this time. We will send a calabash to them, with promises of sending more as soon as they finish with the cooking."

He sat down. The fons nodded with satisfaction and simultaneously showed their cups, which Abanda respectfully filled with *Raffia* wine.

Forkon called for Ngoh. "Go and get a large calabash from that room and carry it to your mothers. You can begin serving your fathers." The last words were addressed to Nyanga, who had been standing near the pot of wine. The boy started out and filled the eagerly held out horns. As he was pouring wine into Gyam's horn, Nyanga shook with laughter. Gyam's tongue was continuously running over his lips. What a big horn for such a small man, the boy thought. As he made to move on, Gyam caught his wrist as he emptied the contents of his horn again.

"Don't laugh, my child," Gyam said, tapping the sole of his right foot lightly on the ground. "You know that some people expose themselves to the heat of the sun more than others. Some of us have been more busy than others, and it is just reasonable that we regain some of our spent energy so we can cope with the events to come yet. You know, my boy, that—"

"You will not keep us in suspense, will you?" Mukom complained. Nyanga had been attracted by Gyam's talking and had interrupted his work. Now he hurried over to fill the other horns.

"But our horns are still empty, young man," Gyam called out, his hand outstretched. Those near him laughed mockingly, but that did not bother him.

Awah was uncomfortable. He tapped Gyam lightly on the back. "Don't behave like that. You may give the impression that you wished such a thing to happen so as to create the chance for you to quench your thirst."

Gyam lowered his voice as he answered, "Others will quench theirs at my death. Why shouldn't I quench mine when others depart?"

Awah ignored him and drank from his cup. He thought to himself that the best way to stop Gyam from misbehaving was to change the conversation.

"Chaah. If all the wine tapped here is like this," he said, holding up his horn, "then the Ngwokwong men can begin to think of winning over our daughters." There was general laughter around him.

"You forget one thing. Your young men hang around here because of our incomparable daughters." Gyam spoke excitedly. He forgot for a moment that his horn was empty. Awah raised his horn to his lips, and Gyam was reminded.

"Come and fill your father's horn," he called out. Nyanga filled the horn. Gyam turned round on his chair and faced Awah.

"You Zang people can boast of palm oil. But as we all know, our women ... h'mmm! ... are special." He drank a little from his horn.

Mukom joined the conversation. "You are both wasting words." His voice was resonant. "You are all aware of the fact that the fathers of your fathers got married to our pretty daughters. They were not only beautiful but they were hard-working – so that, in those days, a man from Ngwokwong, Zang, or Etwii who did not marry a woman from Tugi was considered as unlucky. Believe me."

He wetted his lips. Gyam shifted uneasily on his stool and made to speak, but Mukom was talking again.

"I quite agree with Gyam that your daughters are pretty. But from what I just said, the honour comes right back to us, the Tugi people." He smiled and swelled with importance, like one who had his opponents in a tight corner.

"Ha!" Egwendu, from Etwii, jumped in, "Hearing you, one would think it is a child talking. You don't even seem to realise what you have been saying." He added, between bursts of laughter, "Tell me, is it you or your wife that determines the sex of the child to be born?"

Mukom scratched his head, looking for an answer. He heard the general laughter and realised the implication of his words.

At that moment, Fomujang walked in, followed by Mimba and two young men. As the others found seats for themselves, Fomujang moved over to Forkon and informed him that the women were already taking care of the cow meat.

A new jug was emptied into the pot, and the newcomers drew out their horns. The noise in the room had lessened. Gyam was still holding his sides from having laughed so much.

"Fomujang," he called out and started tottering across the room towards him. "Can you imagine a man with at least ten children in his household saying that his wives and not him …" Gyam slapped his thigh and forced himself into the tight space between Fomujang and Mimba. As Fomujang's cup was being filled, he showed his, and Ngoh filled it. "Ha! His wives and not him …" Gyam went on, "who decide on whether their child be a male or female? Will you swallow that?"

Mukom was protesting hotly that he had said nothing of the sort, but the noise in the room drowned his protests. From the smiles on their faces, it was clear that the fons were enjoying the arguments without themselves taking part. They, they knew, represented the solemn part of the day's events.

The food was ready. Two women entered the room carrying between them a long, wide wooden bowl. It was full of plantain porridge and vegetables. They placed the bowl close to the pot of wine. A third woman came in carrying a relatively smaller bowl, which she placed in front of the fons. The men went one after the other and picked a plantain and carried a handful of vegetables. This was considered the ideal food after consuming a good amount of *Raffia* wine.

The sun was beginning to disappear behind the hills. The cold announced its arrival as children started sneezing noisily outside. The women gathered wood into several heaps, ready to put them on fire when the cold became unbearable. Back in the hall, the men talked generally as they filled their stomachs with wine and food.

At the corner where he sat, Akatcho did not appear to be taking part in the eating and drinking. He sat staring into his horn and yet not seeing its contents. His mind went back to Zang. Fomujang and Awah had been very close friends since their childhood days. They had always helped each other and worked for their mutual benefit. A year before, Awah had stayed a week in Ngwokwong and helped to bush-clear Fomujang's yam farm.

When the year went round and the farming season arrived, Fomujang prepared to leave for Zang. But at that time the fon fell ill, and according to the laws of the land, no elder could leave the village at such a crucial moment, until there were signs of improvement. Akatcho had gone ahead to inform Awah of the reason for his father's delay. Fomujang and Gyam had joined him five days later, only to leave in a hurry after a night's stay.

Akatcho relived in his mind the few days before his father's arrival in Zang. Angye had taken him around the village. It was during one of such walks that he had met Nande. She was one of those rare girls with the powerful combination which most men admire and which most women envy: beauty and hard work. After their first meeting, nothing was more interesting for both boys other than meeting and conversing with Nande.

Akatcho made up his mind. He must talk to his father about her. After all, was his chin not beginning to grow dark with strands of black hair?

Someone coughed noisily near him. He started and realised that he had not even tested the wine in his horn. He looked round and saw his father in conversation with Awah. He moved across towards them and asked after Angye. He was eager to learn the latest news about Nande.

"I have no news, my son," Awah answered, "but his junior brother, Muki, brought the wine. He says that Angye was invited by Tifang to help repair the fence of his pig."

The young man shivered slightly. Tifang was Nande's father. Akatcho wished he were there to help him perform the task. That would have brought him closer to Nande's father. He sighed, moved back to his seat, and raised his horn to his lips for the first time.

Night was coming quickly. The women went behind the compound to cut plantain leaves. These they spread on the bare floor and flung themselves on, completely exhausted.

The Fon of Zang whispered something into Forkon's ear. The latter stood up. "*Sssh*. Listen, valiant sons of their fathers. Our father from Zang has a word for us."

The fon slowly bent, and tilting his right leg outwards, he placed the curved bottom of his cow horn beneath. He brought back his foot to hold the horn steady. He then straightened in his chair, cleared his throat, and seemed to await the inevitable answer.

"Mbeeeh."

"I don't have much to say. I just want to remind you of the saying of our fathers of long ago. Today is not like yesterday; neither will it be the same as tomorrow, yet the demands of the body remain the same. By this our ancestors meant that if you drink all your wine and eat all your food today, you will be running the risk of not responding positively to your bodily demands tomorrow. We would go back to our homes now with the intention of coming back on the day that will be revealed for your father to return. Stay well, my children."

He picked up his horn, emptied the dregs on the ground, and gave it to his *chinda* to drop into the bag. The three fons walked out onto the yard and were soon joined by their close collaborators. Most of the visitors remained behind to spend the traditionally accepted three days of mourning in Ngwokwong.

Many did not fall asleep until the early hours of the morning.

Chapter 5

Ngwokwong's *Raffia* wine was very much longed for in the neighbouring villages. If a stranger stood at the top of the hills surrounding Ngwokwong and looked down at the valley, he/she would not believe that there existed human life. The *Raffia* palm bush was so dense that only the smoke that escaped through into the atmosphere could indicate the position of the grass-roofed huts or farms. The houses were built of bamboo from the *Raffia* palms. Every compound was enclosed by a forest of plantain and cocoyam plants, both of which were staple foods of the people.

A new type of plant was already growing around many of the compounds but was not being noticed yet. This was later known as the sisal plant. It was many moons ago that the plant had been introduced in the village. The fon had been contacted by a stranger at Tad market, the largest market, in which strangers from distant lands came to sell salt and soap and to buy palm oil and drink palm and *Raffia* wine. The stranger had offered some seeds to the fon.

"If you take these seeds to your people, and they grow them well, then great things will you gain," the stranger had said.

"Great things will come from what? From these dried little leaves?" the astonished fon had asked, feeling the lightness of the seeds.

"No, no," the stranger had said hurriedly, "the great things will not come from these little things in my hands or from what they will turn into. Come with me into that hut, and I will tell you the secret."

The fon had noted how badly the man spoke the language. He had dragged himself rather than walked with the man, for his mind was doubtful.

The little hut was full of the strong odour of palm and *Raffia* wine. There were hardly any empty seats. The fon had coughed twice to attract attention. The black fibrous cap with a red feather stuck in it, the carved stick, and the long, marked robe identified him. There was a rapid movement as the men in the room quickly created ample space for the newcomers.

The fon sat down on his special stool placed for him by his *chinda*. "May I know who you are and where you come from?" he asked.

"I come from a big place called Menda. I work there, and I have been studying your language for a long time so that I can come and reveal this secret to you."

All smiles, the stranger had called for two jugs of wine, and as they drank, he laboriously explained how the growing of sisal was to be carried out.

"When these seeds become full-grown plants, they will protect your compounds, farms, and animals from wildfire. They will also stop animals from destroying crops in the farms. And that will reduce the fighting that could result between farmers and animal owners. Where I come from, many families have suffered the loss of their homes and crops to wildfire and animals respectively. Many lives are lost in the struggle to protect property and livelihoods. You are a wise man, as I can see, and you definitely want your people to live in peace."

"Is there any plant that can stop wildfire in its tracks?" the fon had asked, amused, as he was convinced that such a plant did not exist.

"You will discover it yourself when the plants have grown," the stranger said with conviction. "I do not want to see the destruction that has happened in my own land to be repeated in other peace-loving villages. This is my own contribution to building a peaceful world."

After giving the fon a good quantity of sisal seeds, he had bade him farewell and had left to make new contacts. As soon as he had returned from Tad, the fon had summoned his councillors, and the matter had been discussed. They had come to the conclusion that each household was to plant twenty seeds and to take care of them until such a time that the great things would come out from them.

Three families lived at the summit of the three main hills that surrounded Ngwokwong. These were the *Bororos*. They were herdsmen who, after travelling for long distances in search of land to settle with their livestock, had arrived at Ngwokwong and gotten favour from the fon. The natives looked at the *Bororo*s as a queer race, for their lives were inextricably linked to their livestock. They did little farming and fed essentially on milk and corn, the main crop around their huts. They lived in round huts with roofs that extended to the ground. From a distance, the huts looked like huge anthills.

They generally could speak meta, the language of their host, after many years of living on Ngwokwong land. The oldest of them was called Lamu. He had been the first to arrive Ngwokwong, almost forty years back, and had found favour with the fon. The latter had allowed him and his family to settle in the hill behind the mighty rock that carried his name. Lamu arrived from the east with one wife and a daughter, and he married two more times while in Ngwokwong. The other two wives were the daughters of the two families that arrived at Ngwokwong a few years after him. With his three wives, he had eleven children.

Often, after a tiring day with his herd of cattle, Lamu would descend into Fomujang's compound, which was at the foot of the hill on which he dwelled. When he began his long descent, the sun would just be starting to show its red glow in the horizon.

This day, unlike on previous days, he did not sing as he approached the compound. The recent event might mark a turning point in his life. His mind was troubled. At his age, he did not want to think of making another long and uncertain journey onto unknown lands. Yesterday he had parted with a cow. That should convince the people of Ngwokwong of his compassion. The three *Bororo* families each parted with a cow every three years as a mark of their gratitude for the land given them. Now, a new fon could mean new terms and possibly new lands. It was only when he was making his way amongst the plantain stems surrounding Fomujang's compound that he realised he might be too early to meet anybody at home. He raised his head and tilted his broad fibre sun cap. No smoke came from the house. He hesitated, shrugged, and moved on. He reached the back of the hut and went right to the front. To his relief and surprise, he saw Tengu just lowering a basket of cocoyam to the ground.

He coughed dryly. The basket that was already near the ground fell out of Tengu's hands. She swung round and then heaved a sigh of relief. She was a woman in her middle age. Her regular face still carried traces of her maidenly beauty. She was Fomujang's first and only wife.

"Aah, Lamu. It is you?" Her voice was small.

"Aah. You are just returning from the farm. I thought I would be too early today. Where is Muyang?"

Tengu opened the door and moved in. "Muyang branched off along the way to see her friend Ijang, who has been ill for the last three days," she answered him.

Lamu was just about to cross the threshold when footsteps sounded behind him. He looked with admiration as Muyang came along the path, swaying gently to the rhythm of a tune she was humming. There was a small basket containing yams fixed on her head. She was slim and well proportioned. She was Fomujang's only daughter. She came up to Lamu and broke into a smile.

"Chaah! Lamu, why don't you ever bring Amina with you? Lamu admired the deep curves of her cheeks and the even set of teeth.

"It looks like I have to keep answering the same question every day," Lamu said, responding to the girl's smile. "I have been out all day with my cows."

"But I can see that you were not with the cows today. You are earlier than usual," Muyang argued on. Lamu crossed the threshold, pulled a stool to his side, and sat down. Tengu had already lit the fire and was peeling the cocoyams.

"That is true today, my daughter." Lamu's face instantly became serious. "I came earlier to get details of what happened yesterday."

"*Wooh!* Do not mention it again." Tengu raised her head. "With the fon gone, I do not know what Ngwokwong will become, since his only grown son roams about like one afflicted by the wandering sickness".

"Where is Fomujang?" Lamu asked.

44

"I believe he left this morning for tawh."

"What about Akatcho?" Lamu looked at Muyang, expecting an answer from her.

The young girl clapped her hands and twisted her mouth in a mocking gesture. "H'mmm, that one! He told me yesterday that he was going to Zang along with the Zang people. He also said that he would be back today. Well, he is not back yet. If I was the one that stayed out this long, father would only kill me." Muyang pushed her lips forward and threw back her head. Her hands folded over her breasts. That meant she was getting angry.

Tengu looked hurt. She loved her daughter. She also knew that she was too lenient with her, to a fault. However, what could she do? Muyang was her only daughter. She looked with reproach at her. "Why do you keep comparing yourself with your brother? I have always told you that your brother is a man, and you are a woman. Will you give me the big pot, please?"

The young girl rose from her seat, stormed into the only inner room of the hut, and burst into tears.

Lamu did not like such scenes. He attempted to reason with Muyang. "Wallai! Muyang! That is no good behaviour. Young and strong as you are, you should be helping your mother, instead of …". He left his phrase unfinished and instead shook his head sorrowfully.

"Let her cry," Tengu said calmly. "Our mothers used to say that the best all-round medicine for a woman is her tears." She stepped to one corner of the hut and picked up the pot she needed. Lamu shifted his stool closer to the fireside and spread his long fingers over the flames.

"Our girls these days—" Tengu was saying as she raised the pot onto the red-hot burning wood, but she stopped as footsteps sounded outside.

"Aboh! Come out quickly, or else your father will find you there." Aboh was a flattering name that meant "mother". The girl reappeared quickly and began to look around for something to do.

"Do not bother yourself. Could you fetch some water from the stream?"

The room darkened as Fomujang stood in the doorway, trying to adjust his view of the interior. "Ah, Lamu, you are already there?" he said. Then he saw Muyang and the traces of tears still on her cheeks. "Have you been crying?"

The girl hurried out of the hut with a calabash and went in the direction of the stream.

Fomujang, like Forkon, was a respected councillor of Ngwokwong in his mid-forties. He was a very influential member of the village council. He was married to Tengu, and they had two children, Akatcho and Muyang. He was not a very stern man. There was, however, something about him that always sent a chill up Muyang's spine, particularly when she was naughty. He entered the inner room in which his daughter had been crying earlier and returned with a calabash of *Raffia* wine. He sat opposite to Lamu and poured some wine into his horn. Lamu followed the example. After two gulps of the wine, Fomujang passed his tongue over his lips and looked up at his wife.

"Tengu, can you look back at the time when you had your daughter's age?"

"Yes. Why do you ask?" She looked suspiciously at her husband.

"Did you conduct yourself the way she is behaving now?" He stared into his cup.

Tengu's brows gathered as she tried to give some meaning to her husband's question.

"You must realise," he went on, bringing his thoughts into focus, "that if your daughter is acting the way she is now, it is simply because …". He paused.

"She has no sisters to compete with. Yes, you have said so before. Are you trying to lay blame on me?" Tengu looked disturbed.

"No. Not that," Fomujang said quickly. "How can I blame you when the gods have taken their own decision? You do not understand my point. I simply meant to say that Muyang has come of age." He raised his horn to his lips.

A little silence followed as each person in the room considered his words.

"Wallai! That is quite true," Lamu said, breaking the silence. "I have also noted the changes in her body, as well as behaviour. Your conclusion is very correct, Fomujang." He raised his long eyebrows at Tengu. "Do you not think so, Muyang's mother?"

Tengu clapped her palms and said, "You men have your own eyes."

"Ah ha! If Gyam were here, he would have agreed with me too." Fomujang spread his right palm upwards, sure he was right.

"Where is he? Did I not hear him say he was going with you this morning to visit your traps?" Tengu asked as she arranged the logs of wood under her pot.

"I left him at tawh. You know he will not be here before the jugs of wine there have all been emptied."

"So you are just from tawh?" Lamu shifted on his stool. He needed information.

"Eh, h'mmm. Forkon sent for me early this afternoon. I went together with Gyam. We learnt that Tita has returned. Other elders joined us in tawh."

Shaking his head slowly, Fomujang added, "You will not believe that even at the point of succeeding his father, this young man shows not the least interest in our laws and traditions. I fear tomorrow."

"But did the old man not say something about his succession before he died?" Tengu asked.

"Who knew that he would die?" Fomujang clasped his palms and upturned them in a gesture of helplessness. "He was showing signs of improvement, and that is why I left for Zang. But as Forkon told us yesterday, when the illness became very serious, the old man tried in vain to say something. He passed away with no word crossing his lips."

"But at Ba-yoh's burial, Forkon spoke of the fon's last words," Tengu wondered aloud.

"What else was he to do? Come to think of it, that is certainly what he would have said if he had been able to speak."

48

There was a soft knock on the door. Gyam walked in, followed by Muyang. Tengu rose and helped her daughter with the calabash of water she was carrying. She then opened the pot on the fire and poured some water into it. Gyam made his way silently to the fireside and spread his fingers over the pot.

"You would not believe it, but the cold outside can snatch away one's ears." He sneezed as he inhaled pepper from the cooking pot. "How long has this pot been cooking?" Gyam rubbed his stomach and grinned at Tengu.

"Do not worry. It will soon be ready. It is just your favourite." Then, pointing at his stomach, she remarked, "I have always told you not to fill this with wine before you have eaten."

"Aah! You remind me!" Gyam said excitedly. "Did you hear the story of Nyipi's death?" He looked expectantly at those in the room.

"Tell us what you have in mind," Lamu said.

Gyam was not one to be hurried. He plunged his hand into his little bag and drew out his version of a horn. "You know," he explained, like one unravelling a complex problem, "it is not advisable to talk with dry lips and a dry throat."

Fomujang filled the horns of the two men.

"Walking from tawh to this compound is not a child's play." Gyam filled his horn again. Fomujang was about to say something. Gyam sensed what his friend was preparing to say. He quickly added, "I have always said it. You, Fomujang, are equalled by none as far as this is concerned." He held up his horn and pointed at its contents.

All in the room began to laugh. They all were quite used to Gyam's sense of humour. This little man had lost his wife almost immediately after they had been married. This was enough to change the course of his life. Before his wedding, Gyam had been a man of principle and decision. Everything he did then had had a purpose and plan. He had not been given to drinking. Seldom had he been a talker, but in him had burned the desire and hope of one day rising to one of the most respected positions in the land. His wife's death had come without warning. She had only complained of stomach ache, and before the medicine man was called in, she had passed on. Life for Gyam thereafter became a sort of illusion. He saw the world around him as a place where people went about with empty dreams and ambitions. He often wondered aloud if one could enjoy the fruit of his (her) labour when death, the uninvited guest in all homes and families, lurked around the corners and in the shadows. The death of his dear wife was to him the end of purpose and ambition. He shared out all his land, giving the largest piece to Tengu, the closest friend to his late wife. There was no blood relationship between him and Fomujang, but between the two men existed deep and true love.

Here he was, wifeless, childless, and yet loved by many. That was enough to provide him with the strength to live on and tend to his *Raffia* palms, the only property he had not parted with. He enjoyed good company.

"Well, I know of two women only who can make a man cut his finger." He shot a knowing look at Tengu. The three men impatiently waited for the hot vapour from the food in front of them to disappear. Gyam had attempted twice to pick out a cocoyam from the bowl but found they were still too hot for his fingers. He sat quietly for a while, and then, as suddenly as one who has just been struck with a new idea, he sat upright.

"Pour some more wine here." He showed his horn, and Tengu refilled it.

"Ha! You may not believe me, but I can tell you that this wine can cool this hot food." He smiled as the others raised eyebrows at him.

"Chaah! You do not mean to pour it into the bowl, I hope?" Tengu wondered.

Gyam laughed aloud. "I am no child to do such a thing. Just watch me." He raised his horn to his lips and sipped in some wine. He held the liquid in his mouth. Then he picked a piece of cocoyam and added it to the wine. He swirled the mixture in his mouth and then started to chew. Then he smiled at the others.

"Well," Fomujang said as he bent to select a piece of cocoyam for himself, "all children know that trick. But for elderly ones like ourselves, elderly methods have to be applied."

"And I believe 'elderly method' means letting the food cool off naturally, eh?" Lamu added as his hand plunged into the bowl.

Gyam was not admitting defeat. "When shall elders admit that some children's ideas are better than theirs?"

"What do you mean by that?" Fomujang asked with interest. He never underestimated his friend's intelligence.

"I know of a man who lost his life because another man who could help just let nature take its course." Gyam looked very serious as he explained further. "we must try to make things happen the way we want to see them – otherwise, the future will shape itself and not necessarily in our favour."

Tengu thought Gyam was alluding to his late wife, and her face twisted in pain. Gyam realised what Tengu was thinking and quickly added, "I am not talking about my unfortunate wife."

"Are you just trying to explain yourself out of your recent childish act, or are you building a story?" Lamu was not happy that Gyam altered the conversation from the subject that could clarify some of his concerns. What was happening in Ngwokwong could have a direct impact on his future.

"What do you mean about building up a story?" Gyam's brows gathered. Do you not remember how Nyipi met his fate? Nyipi of Etwii?"

Fomujang frowned. He saw no link between that fatal incident and their present discussions.

"Everyone knows that Nyipi died by accident. Of course no one could have stopped the grass giving way under his weight," he remarked.

"Ah ha! I heard of that sorrowful event but got nothing as to how it happened," Lamu said eagerly. He was getting back into the conversation with interest.

"I have heard two or three versions of that sad event. I do not know which is true," Tengu complained.

Gyam noisily licked his fingers, poured more wine into his horn, and pulled away from the bowl towards the fireside.

"You all seem to have got little or nothing of what really happened with that poor man's death." He made himself comfortable and sipped from his horn before continuing to speak.

"Listen. I went to Etwii during the funeral celebration and got the details from Tayou, who saw Nyipi die with his own two eyes. This is what he told me. Nyipi and he had left early one morning to go hunting. After a half-day's journey in the forest, they found out with disgust that most of their traps had failed. On their way home, they stopped near the stream at Tonokwo to examine the last trap. They found a huge antelope caught in the trap and the wire cut deep into its flesh. It was too heavy for the two of them to carry back home. They agreed that Tayou should run back home for help. The clouds were beginning to gather fast, and he moved quickly. He crossed the Tonokwo stream as the first drops of rain came down. The water reached above his knees. By the time he reached his compound, the rain was falling heavily. He invited two of his younger brothers to follow him with large bags. He turned and began to hurry back as he shouted to them to hasten and meet him at the stream. He hoped that he and Nyipi could pull the animal across the stream before it overflowed its banks. Just as he reached the stream, he caught sight of his friend at the edge of the fast-flowing water, pulling hard at the animal. He noted with dismay how much the water had risen. He raised his voice and shouted to Nyipi not to attempt crossing. The latter pulled on his ear to show he did not understand what the other was saying. As Tayou began shouting to reiterate his point, Nyipi edged dangerously close to the edge of the slope. Tayou made frantic gestures to his friend to move back. Nyipi moved his right leg sideways and unfortunately stepped on a loose stone. In the next instant, he was lying on the slope holding to some grass as his legs floated in the water. He shouted to Tayou to get some rope and throw it to him. Tayou shouted back that in attempting to catch the rope, he could fall into the stream. As the other two boys arrived at the scene, the grass gave way, and Nyipi disappeared into the dark water. You know the rest."

Gyam raised his right leg, rested it on a log of wood, and sipped from his horn. He gave the others time to digest his story.

"Chaah!" Tengu clapped her hands in sorrow. "What a horrible way for a young man to die."

After some silence, Fomujang calmly observed with a wan smile, "I thought you were trying to relate the story to our previous conversation?"

Gyam did not hide his disappointment. "You still do not get it? You do not see that Tayou could have saved Nyipi? Even a child could have seen that the grass was not going to hold out for long. Nyipi himself got the idea of a rope. If there was no rope, there are bamboos everywhere. Had he thrown one to Nyipi, the latter could have been pulled across."

"If Tayou could not save his friend's life, how does that clarify our earlier discussion?" Fomujang insisted calmly though very eager to see his friend's point.

Gyam shrugged his shoulders. He beat the air with his index finger. "Tayou could have saved Nyipi." He wetted his lips and then continued, "But he let nature follow its course. I was very hungry, and hunger kills. There was food in front of me. Was I to wait for the food to cool naturally and die of hunger or devise the means to save my stomach and my life?"

As the others burst out laughing, he added, "It may seem childish, but the trick saved my life."

The night was advancing quickly. Lamu climbed the hill towards his hut. He was worried. The young man who might succeed the late fon might not make life easy for him and his friends. He wondered what the future held for him and his family.

Chapter 6

By the time the cock crowed for the second time, Fomujang was already in his palm bush. Tengu and Muyang had also left early for their farm. There was a lot of weeding to do. The sun was just beginning to send its first rays when Fomujang walked back into his compound, two large calabashes suspending at each end of a bamboo pole placed across his shoulders. He looked for his bowl of food where Tengu always kept it. He carried it outside and then brought out his smaller calabash of wine. He sat down and began to enjoy his meal. He remembered that he had to repair the fence for his pig. Recently Munya's pig had been speared to death for destroying Andang's wife's potato farm. Who had done the killing, nobody knew. After the impending ceremony to mark the beginning of the return of the fon, the council would look into that. But he, Fomujang, was not going to give the chance for his pig to be shot at and killed.

He looked up. The sun was beginning to move faster across the sky. He would try to mend the fence before Gyam called on him. He knew his friend would be impatient for them to leave on their errand. He was just raising his horn to his lips when Akatcho came up the path.

"Father, how did your day break?" he greeted him.

"How could you have left for Zang without telling me, my son?"

Akatcho drew nearer and found a seat for himself.

"Have you eaten?" Fomujang asked, looking at the only cocoyam left in his bowl.

"Father, I have something to tell you." Akatcho was staring at the ground. Something touched his arm. He looked up and accepted his father's horn. He poured the contents down his throat, and it seemed to give him courage.

"What is it you want to tell me, my son?"

Fomujang looked closely at his son. This was the first time, he told himself, that the boy had ever shown nervousness in speaking to him.

"Father, h'mmm … eh, during my … my …". Akatcho was stammering badly.

"Look here, my son." Fomujang was irritated. His only male offspring must not in any way show weakness. "You know that I don't like you to behave like a woman," he told him. Then he asked, "Have you met a girl?"

Akatcho nodded.

"Who is she?" Fomujang's tone showed he was unperturbed.

"Nande, Tifang's daughter."

Fomujang closed his eyes as he tried to recollect the girl's features.

Then he slowly nodded. "You have good eyes, my son. She is pretty."

After a brief silence, he added, "You know nothing yet of her character. That, of course, is the vital thing to know about any wife-to-be."

"Yes. That, too, I have studied, Father," Akatcho said excitedly; inwardly he was beaming at the way his father had taken his declaration.

"That is not the way to study a woman's character, my son. I insist on character, because some women put on the best they can when they meet a young man like you. However, when you have taken them to wife, they turn into a nightmare. Our fathers used to say that a bird's bright feathers hide dirty flesh."

"But Father, she is not the type of person to put on a dual character."

"Anyway, I will be leaving for Zang this evening," Fomujang told his son. "I have to tell the Fon of Zang that we will be celebrating our father's life on *ko'o*. Such messages are normally supported with a jug of wine. You may help carry the wine, and in turn we shall pay a courtesy visit to Tifang and your, eh, Nande."

Akatcho smiled. He said excitedly, "You will see that I made a unique choice father. What about Gyam? Won't he come with us?"

"Where to, my boy?" a voice nearby asked.

They both turned to see Gyam adjusting his *Raffia* bag. On his right shoulder he carried a large calabash of *Raffia* wine.

"Of course to Zang. Did I not notify you about it?" Fomujang asked.

"Oh-ho! I thought you were referring to some other place. You will just add a little more wine to this to obtain a jug." Akatcho transferred the calabash onto his own shoulder and carried it into the hut.

"That is very kind of you. Is it fresh, or has it been in the house for some time?"

"Ah! It has been in the house for two days. That is just the right type for real men." He added in an undertone, "It may be too strong for those Zang people, though. If you mix it with a little fresh wine, I do not see the Zang woman who would not give you anything you ask for, with the exception of eh … eeh."

"Stop your insinuation. I am going to do the mixing." Fomujang moved into the hut. He emerged some minutes later with a calabash. Gyam took his horn out and tested the wine. He nodded approvingly.

"This is good. But if it stays till morning, it will lose its flavour."

The two men drank as they talked about the past events. Fomujang looked up at the sky. The sun was almost directly overhead. He promised himself to tend to his pig's fence immediately they returned from their trip to Zang.

"We could leave now. I have told Tengu of my intended journey – except that I will visit Tifang as well."

"Tifang?" Gyam did not believe he had heard correctly.

"I will inform you on the way," Fomujang said calmly.

Akatcho came out of the house with a jug of wine. The three men got ready and left on their errand.

As the sun disappeared over the horizon, the three men walked into the fon's palace at Zang. This village was more populated and had a bigger surface area than its neighbours. The fon, as if in recognition of these facts, was married to eight wives. No neighbouring fon had more than six wives.

Carefully, Akatcho lowered the jug to the ground. They all stood at the entrance to the reception hall, waiting for someone to receive them. The little children in the compound had seen them come and had rushed off to their mothers' huts to inform them. Six of the women were at home. They came out of the huts one after the other and moved towards the strangers. As they recognised who the three men were, they burst out with questions about the happenings in Ngwokwong.

The eldest of the women stepped ahead of the others. "Chaah! Baba Fomujang. You are lucky that the night did not catch up with you. How are Tengu and my daughter Muyang?"

"They are doing fine. The only news is what you already know."

The woman turned to the youngest of the other five women. "Nyoh, help my son with the jug." She bowed slightly to the men, and they followed her into the spacious room.

As they found stools for themselves, she said, "Once again, welcome to you all. You will not have long to wait, because it has been quite some time now since the fon went into his palm bush. Give me just a few minutes to fetch something for you to calm your hunger and quench your thirst." She turned and hurried to the door.

"Aboh," Gyam called out, "you must have noticed my silence since our arrival here. I have not even enquired about my child's health. How is Tah?"

"His fever has left him, and he has gone into the bush with his friends." The woman felt that Gyam had something else to say. As she turned to go, she saw Gyam grip his throat.

59

"My throat is so dry and really hurts as I speak." He closed his eyes and swayed rhythmically from side to side, his hands on his throat.

The other two laughed, while the woman clapped her hands and went outside smiling. Akatcho's eyes had been exploring the room. He stopped laughing when a strange object came into sight.

"Father, what is that?"

The others followed the direction of his finger to the skeletal head of a gorilla suspended on the wall. In tawh hall in Ngwokwong, Akatcho had noticed various skeletal decorations suspending from the walls. Here in tawh hall at Zang he noted the presence of the same types of decorations, with the one exception of the gorilla skull. The fon's stool stood directly below the skull. Curious designs were carved on the stool, the top of which was covered with a gorilla skin.

Fomujang shifted slightly on his chair. "My son," he said, keeping his voice low, "you will not find that type of skull elsewhere. It is the unique symbol of originality and power. Ngwokwong, Tugi, and many other neighbouring villages are direct descendants of Zang. In the beginning, all was one land, one people, and one powerful fon. However, there came a time when brothers fought for the fondom of Zang. There were many unsuccessful attempts to regain peace, but none of the brothers was willing to back down. The inevitable consequence was that each one of the brothers left with a small group of followers and settled in the sites where we have the different villages today." He broke off his narration as the woman returned, followed by Nyoh.

"I will finish the tale at home. You must remind me." Akatcho nodded.

The woman came nearer. Gyam's horn was already out and held forward. Nyoh paused in front of Fomujang as the latter took out his horn from his bag. He turned it and hit the open end against his palm. That was to clear out any dirt in it.

"Go ahead and serve my friend, good woman. You can see that he is very thirsty." Nyoh moved over to Gyam.

"Did you clean your cup?" Fomujang asked, quite amused with the serious look on his friend's face.

"My cup never stores dirt. Let us taste this and see if the Zang people are good tappers."

Nyoh filled the cup. As the woman moved over to Fomujang, Gyam's cup was pointing at her again. She looked at the size of the horn and stifled a whistle.

"Do not wait, please. I have only made things worse by taking one round and stopping there."

He drank two rounds again before a sigh of relief escaped his throat. Amused, he looked at Akatcho, who was still on his first round. He placed his palm on the boy's knee.

"When you shall attain my age, you will then understand why I need to drink more wine than you do. You are still very fresh, and much water circulates in your body. That is why there is very little space for wine inside your body." He covered his lips with his horn.

The elderly woman had placed a bowl of hot cocoyam porridge, rich in bitterleaf vegetable, in front of the men. Akatcho and his father were already helping themselves from the bowl, while Gyam contented himself with filling his horn and talking to the woman. She said, "If only you will eat a little of those leaves in the bowl."

"Oh no! Do you think the leaves have the same effect as kola nuts? They have the same taste, no doubt, but—"

Fomujang showed his surprise. "What are you saying, Gyam?"

"Do you mean you have forgotten or just felt like neglecting our tradition?" Gyam shifted uneasily on his stool.

"I did not mean what you think. I was just hoping that the right moment should come. In fact, I—"

He stopped as the room darkened. The fon stood for a moment in the doorway, trying to accustom his eyes to the light inside the room. It took a few moments before he could identify the visitors. Slowly he stepped in and moved to his seat. The three men rubbed their palms together and clapped slowly in unison.

"Mbeeeh." They uttered the traditional salute.

"Have you come well, my children?" the fon responded.

Fomujang lightly touched his son and glanced at the jug they had brought. The boy stood up and went across the room to where Nyoh had placed the jug. He carried it to the fon and placed it before him. The fon looked significantly at his eldest wife and nodded twice.

She left the room. She was the fon's first wife, and according to tradition, she was hardly referred to or called by her name. Reference to her was made in connection to her child or husband.

No one spoke until she came back with five carefully selected kola nuts and presented them to Fomujang.

The latter broke three of them into nine pieces. He moved over to the fon and respectfully presented the pieces of kola nut in his open palms to the fon. The latter selected two pieces and nodded his thanks. Fomujang let the others select a piece of kola nut each before taking his seat again. The fon's eldest wife went into an inner room and quickly returned with a black horn and a round-bottomed calabash. She filled the horn and carried it in both palms to her husband. He held the horn in front of himself for a while, as if scrutinising its contents. Then he stood up, walked to the door, and sprinkled the wine in a circular pattern on the threshold. That gesture was believed to send away evil spirits. He walked back to his seat.

"Son of Azah, my son, come and drink from your father's horn." The fon spoke abruptly.

Fomujang moved quickly across the room, stooped respectfully before the fon, and accepted the horn in both palms. He raised the royal horn to his lips and emptied its contents. He then returned it and moved back to his seat.

The woman filled the fon's horn again and moved over to the others. When all horns had been filled, the fon broke the silence. "If what I think is right, then you are here to inform me of your decision as regards the celebration marking the return of your father."

"Mbeeeh. That is exactly why we are here. Ko'o has been designated as the day when everybody will come out and let the earth shake in memory of our father and expectation of his return."

The fon thought for a while and then nodded. "You have chosen well. For no other day would have suited us. Anyway, you do not intend to go back to Ngwokwong this night, do you?"

"Oh no!" Fomujang answered quickly. "How can a man enter his own house and want to sleep outside?"

The fon smiled. "I am glad with what you say," he said with satisfaction. "I will send for some of my elders, and we will make this evening a memorable one."

"If you would not mind it much," Fomujang said, "we intended to visit Awah and Tifang. You see, our father went on his long journey while I was here arranging our farm work. I just thought that, as I have come again, I may go and greet them before we come back and share some palm wine with the elders."

"Ah! That is a good thing to do. Did not our long-gone fathers say that greeting is the gum that holds people and villages together? By the time you are back, some of my elders shall be waiting for you."

For the third time Gyam knocked on Tifang's door.

"Who is there?" came a deep voice from behind the door.

"Ngwokwong," Gyam replied, smiling at those behind him.

"Who?" Tifang asked in astonishment.

"Calm your nerves, brother. Are you sure you aren't expecting a visitor from Ngwokwong?" Gyam asked.

By now Tifang had recognised his guest's voice. "Is that you, Gyam?"

The door was thrown wide open, and the three men walked in.

"Engoneb," Tifang called, looking towards the inner room, "come and see who we have here!"

A woman with a heavy torso came into the room. "You are welcome! What could have brought you this far at such a time?"

Tifang scowled his wife. "They have not even sat down."

Gyam sat on a stool and looked up at the woman. "Tell me, aboh, does a squirrel know how to select the palm tree from which to pick its palm nuts? But where is the pride of this house?"

Tifang misunderstood Gyam's words. "Please do not be angry at Engoneb's carelessness. She should not have asked questions as if you are strangers, he pleaded. It is just—"

"I think your mind is going up the wrong tree." Fomujang gave them one of his rare smiles. "If I get my friend correctly, by 'pride of the house' he is referring to Nande. Is it not, Gyam?"

"Where is my daughter?" Gyam asked, looking past Engoneb, who stood with hands on her cheeks as though saying she were sorry.

Tifang placed a jug of wine in front of his guests.

"I will not taste this wine before my daughter comes and greets me." Gyam managed a determined posture.

"Go and get her out of bed," Tifang ordered his wife. "Let her come and greet her fathers."

Akatcho tasted the wine and noted that it was too strong for him. Fomujang drank with apparent satisfaction. He was inwardly glad he had come with Gyam. His friend would introduce the reason for their visit with a lot of ease.

The girl came into the room. She rubbed her eyes with the backs of her hands.

Akatcho began rising from his seat the moment he saw her but quickly arrested his gesture. His heart was skipping slightly. He must not betray his emotions. He watched as Gyam moved across the room and took the girl's hand gently.

"Come, my daughter. Come and greet your father."

She moved over and extended her soft, slender hand into the larger palm of Fomujang. Her hand lingered in Akatcho's as she bit her left fingers and stared at the floor. They both trembled slightly. Akatcho was aware of the eyes on him.

"How are you, Nande?"

"I am well," she replied, her voice hardly audible. Akatcho let go her hand, and she moved over to her mother.

Gyam broke the slight tension that was beginning to steal in. "And now, my dear Tifang," he said, "I can quench my thirst. You do not expect a man in his right mind to move into his house, eat, drink, and relax, when he completely ignores what is irking his daughter."

Tifang looked at Fomujang and raised his brows enquiringly. Fomujang's face clouded faintly as he tried to think of the right words to introduce his topic. Tifang misjudged the frown and said apologetically, "Please do not take it wrongly. However, when a man hears a knock on his door at this time of the night, his wine could go down the wrong way."

Fomujang shifted on his chair, uneasily trying to think of the right proverb. Gyam noticed his difficulty. He cleared his throat, attracting the attention to him.

"After the long and tiring work we had to do these past days, it is only natural that we should feel hungry and thirsty." He showed his empty cup, and Tifang filled it.

"This palm wine has some special flavour. Right from ancient times, our ancestors gave to each village something to prosper in. In this you will see and appreciate the wisdom of our long-gone fathers."

He paused and looked significantly at those in the room. They were all ears. He wetted his lips and continued. "No single village has all it needs. Otherwise, there would not be the interdependence and cooperation which for so long has proved to be the great unifying factor amongst our people. There would not be the desire to visit and chat amongst brothers as we are doing now. Ha! Your palm wine is unique."

Gyam covered his mouth with his horn. Tifang was enjoying Gyam's speech, without having the least idea what the latter was driving at. Gyam was as clever a speaker as he was entertaining.

"Ngwokwong stands out as the greatest producer of plantains. Our hills and valleys are covered with them. Zang is blessed with oil palms. Here I must remark that these palms produce oil and wine. Isn't that a slight edge over her neighbours?"

"But you are—" Tifang started speaking but stopped as Gyam held up his hand.

"I was just talking, you see. Who are we to judge the wisdom of our ancestors? Let's talk of things within our understanding."

Gyam pursued solemnly, "Who in his right mind will eat plantains without the oil that must give it colour and taste?"

Fomujang smiled in his mind. He was following Gyam, all right. On his part, Tifang was nodding with visible blankness.

Fomujang decided to speak in order to give his friend time to arrange his ideas. "You see, brother, we came here to inform the fon of our intention to initiate the return of our father on ko'o – the day no one goes to the farm. It was just right for us, knowing your house to be so near to come and greet and chat."

"That is a very good thing, indeed. Talking with the fons is not as easy and enjoyable as amongst ourselves."

Tifang poured more wine into Fomujang's horn. Gyam was looking in the direction of Engoneb and Nande.

"Palm oil! H'mmm. Who does not see its great effects? Look at my daughter. Her skin is so soft and oily that even I fear to touch it. Well, age is really a mountain of a weight and a fire of a barrier."

He turned on his stool and looked at Akatcho. The young man was making faces at Nande, oblivious to Gyam's amused stare.

"If you drink palm oil from here, my boy, your skin will be as smooth as hers. I mean, from here." He brought his horn to his mouth with a short laugh.

"You will carry some with you to your mother, will you not, my son?" Engoneb asked, looking at Akatcho.

"Well, well, aboh," Gyam said quickly. "You see, we are just using the language of our fathers' fathers. When a plantain is ripe and ready to be eaten, one must look for the right oil to accompany it. Oils differ in colour, taste, and place. It is only reasonable to choose from the right place, the right taste, and the right colour."

Tifang was beginning to get the point. "Have you forgotten our tradition in that regard?" he asked.

"Oh! Not at all," Gyam responded quickly. "We, of course, have great respect for our tradition. If not for the mission we have been assigned, we would not have come so empty-handed. We thought it necessary to take off time from our mission to come and chat and plant the seed."

Tifang looked doubtful and undecided. Fomujang decided to push their idea farther.

"It is a good thing to plant a high-quality seed on good soil. One can only harvest yams where yam seedlings were sown. We hope the seed we plant tonight will have blossomed in your mind by the time we make our real visit. Will the day after ko'o be convenient for you?"

Tifang looked in his wife's direction. She was not there. Nande had folded herself up, her head on her knees. She did not see her father watching her. She continued blinking and putting out her tongue at Akatcho. The latter smiled back at her. That was that, Tifang told himself.

As his wife came into the room, he turned to his guests and slowly nodded. Engoneb moved closer with a small round-bottomed calabash. "You will take this to your mother, my child."

"Thank you, Mother." Akatcho took the calabash of palm oil.

As the three men rose to their feet, the girl darted to an inner room and reappeared instantly with a little tied bundle of leaves. "You will give that to Muyang. It is not much."

"What is it?" Akatcho asked.

"Palm kernels."

"What about me? I have nothing? I will eat up all the kernels."

The girl laughed timidly at Akatcho's false show of anger and darted back gracefully towards her mother.

"Look here," Gyam intervened, tapping Akatcho on the back, "you cannot be that selfish to want to have two things at the same time. The oil is for you and the kernels for Muyang, eh?"

"The oil is for Tengu," Engoneb innocently corrected.

"Well, well," Gyam said throwing up his hands, "oil differs in type and quality. Some we eat with our food, others we drink with our hearts. Nonetheless, his mother will prepare his favourite meal with it, and his mouth will be satisfied with the taste. Though his heart will still—"

"It is getting late. Please get them some sticks to light the way," Tifang urged his wife, deliberately cutting short Gyam's speech. He wanted to be the one to give his wife the idea. He stared at Fomujang, and the latter nodded with understanding and moved towards Nande.

"You will look well after yourself, will you not, my child?" Fomujang placed his big hand on her shoulder. She nodded. Gyam came closer.

"I will want to see you fatter than this when next I come. You promise?" He bent slightly and looked up into the girl's face. She nervously covered her face with her palms and nodded.

Engoneb came in with the burning sticks. Akatcho let the others move ahead. He was alone for a few moments with Nande.

"You will come again?" she asked anxiously.

"Yes, as soon as I can. I will come for you."

Akatcho looked into her eyes and saw the love in them. His right palm lingered on her left cheek then he forced his body away to meet the others.

Chapter 7

The men sat in a wide circle in the small room. A huge clay pot full to the brim with *Raffia* wine stood in its centre. All the councillors had arrived earlier than usual. They were all conversant with the important point on the agenda. They conversed in low tones as they awaited the arrival of Forkon.

Outside, the sun was rapidly withdrawing its bright glow. Forkon looked up at the sinking orb and hoped that he was not very late. He did not want to keep the councillors waiting too long for him. He hurried along the snaky path as quickly as his legs could carry him. The last traces of the sun's red blaze disappeared just as he arrived at the outskirts of the tawh hall. He folded his cloth closely around his body and went round into the room. The men in the room did not need to turn their heads to the door to know who had walked in. Forkon went round to his seat. An unoccupied stool stood between him and Abanda. He sat down and rubbed his palms together, and the others began the uniform clapping that was the traditional salute. As the clapping stopped, Abanda straightened on his seat and cleared his throat.

"Are we ready, great and worthy sons of their fathers?" he asked, searching the faces.

"Yaah," came the unanimous answer.

Abanda faced Forkon. "When is he coming?"

"Any moment now." Forkon drew a deep breath. It was obvious he was still catching his breath.

As if by a known signal, the ten pairs of eyes in the room focused on the empty stool. A sob escaped them, revealing their internal struggle. It was only sometime after the men had resumed their low-toned conversation that Tita made his way into the room. His mother followed him but did not cross the threshold. She stood outside, by the entrance. As the young strolled over to his seat, she turned and moved back to her hut.

Tita sat down, and all eyes focussed on him, expectantly. He just sat and looked blankly ahead. He saw Forkon shaking his head, a sad expression on his face. He slowly turned his eyes and looked at the other men in the room. He saw only disappointment and unhappiness on their faces.

Unenthusiastically, Forkon sat straight on his stool. He remained silent and sullen for some moments before his lips parted.

"My brothers, we must accept the fact that we have a difficult start. Yet we must also realise that nobody becomes a store of wisdom without acquiring it. It is only after building a house to completion that one may move in. How can a bird keep flying under the heat of the sun and the violence of the rains and yet think it is in its nest? No, my brothers! No wisdom comes from nothing. We must learn, respect, and follow what our fathers taught us if we want to be the wise men of our time."

He paused, cleared his throat, and turned slightly towards Tita.

"My dear son. Son of Ngwokwong. You are here amongst your fathers. You are also here amongst those you may soon call your children."

Tita's fingers were uneasily rubbing the few strands of hair under his chin.

"But remember," Forkon said, trying to keep his tone even, "that no son is his father's son, worthy of that title, if he does not acquire his father's wisdom, either by inheritance or guidance. Since your return – finally, we hope it will be – I am sick at heart to bring to your notice that you have paid little or no attention to our tradition and customs. Perhaps your coming and going is responsible for the ignorance you show."

Forkon looked round at the other faces. The men nodded to show he was speaking what was on their minds. He turned again towards Tita and gently pulled at his white beard. The young man quickly withdrew his hand from his chin.

"You have much to learn, my son. Look at your fathers in this room. Do you know each and every one of them?"

Tita nodded confirming he did.

"These are your fathers." Forkon spoke with emphasis. "They will guide you step by step. You have to learn quickly. We have two weeks before the day when Ngwokwong will raise its voice and call on the name of her departed son, your father. Before we proceed to the necessary arrangements, it is the wish of all of us here present to hear from your own lips what you have been doing away from your own land and whether you are prepared to be a true father of Ngwokwong. The gods decided that your elder brother should go with our father on his journey. That leaves us no choice but to groom you and make you fit for your father – our father – to return to us through you."

Forkon raised his brows at Tita and then folded himself down slowly, expecting a reaction from the young man. Tita stood up. His body was well proportioned. He was slightly shorter than Akatcho but had larger biceps and a broader chest. Abanda, particularly, noted the comparison in his mind. Tita passed his tongue several times over his lips. Clearly, he was at a loss how to start.

"My dear fathers," he began, with an effort to keep his voice steady, "since childhood I have developed much interest in hunting, as you may know. I always wanted to be a greater and better hunter than the unfortunate Wunde of our well-known fable. During one of my hunting expeditions, I ventured beyond the hills of Tugi. When I realised I had gone too far, I was about to return, when I came across a herd of cattle. No one seemed to be with them. I moved closer and saw an old and tired *Bororo* man lying under a flat rock. His name is Bassambo. I spoke to him in our language, and he understood me. I told him that … that …".

Tita stopped and looked at the floor, nervously. His mother's words of that morning invaded his mind: "You are incontestably the fon-to-be." He had to show no fear. Forkon thought he saw a sneer in the boy's face as he resumed.

"Well, I told Bassambo that I was an orphan and wanted to earn some cows."

He paused as the men exchanged looks uneasily.

"He had no sons. I offered to stay and assist him in caring for his cattle. In exchange, Bassambo offered to give me a cow after every ten months. Every morning I took the cows to distant places to graze. After I had two cows from Bassambo, he fell ill and, unfortunately, passed away. The leader of the *Bororo*s there, called Musa, shared Bassambo's cows among three other *Bororo* families. I was given four cows out of the lot for the support I had given their brother. Musa invited me to work with him under the same terms as with Bassambo. I earned four cows with Musa.

When I had ten cows, I thought that if I came home with them and gave them to my father, he would forgive my long absence. Not knowing what his reaction would be, I decided to leave the cows with a *Bororo* friend in a place called Menka. I came to tell him first and seek his approval. But when I arrived …".

Tita stopped, and his face looked pale. He controlled his emotions and looked at Forkon. "I have ten cows beyond the hill. When can I go to bring them?"

Forkon gritted his teeth. He spoke slowly but with energy. "You have first got to realise your position in this village. That you are here at this crucial moment is a blessing to our people. How would we explain your absence on ko'o, when people young and old will pour into our land from all the surrounding villages? We are counting on you to uphold the honour and dignity of our people."

Forkon exhaled deeply and looked closely at the young man. He could read the worry on Tita's face. He raised his brows, expecting to hear more.

"Now that everything my father left is in my care, how do I know where to get his sheep and goats, given that my mother doesn't know?" Tita's voice rose slightly.

"How can you try to catch a bird without first trying to spot it, my child? Everything shall be done according to our laws and tradition. Who are we to disregard our tradition? Look here, young man. Do not try to jump across a river wider than your height when a reliable bridge passes over it. You need guidance. Shall we guide you?" Forkon was almost biting each word of his last question.

All eyes in the room settled on the young man, the same question written on each face.

"Yes, my fathers," Tita spoke clearly. "I am willing and prepared to be guided. But please promise to let me go and get my cows."

"After ko'o we will look into that. Menka that you mentioned is many days' journey from here. We do not want you to go out there now and run the risk of compromising the future of this land. It is the gods that prompted your coming home at this time," Abanda said, not masking his impatience.

He looked at Forkon. The latter nodded. He moved to the earthen pot in the centre of the room and picked up the little calabash. He filled it with wine and then moved to the door. He poured some onto the ground and murmured some inaudible words. Then he moved over to Tita. The young man had no horn. Abanda filled his own horn, sipped from it, and handed it to Tita. Forkon's horn was filled next. As Abanda moved over to serve the other elders, Forkon cleared his throat.

"Following today's discussions, I would like to advise our son to begin to look around for the oil with which he will eat his plantains."

Tita looked blank.

"How do you expect him to understand the language of our fathers?" Fomujang asked. Forkon raised his horn to his lips and nodded his head towards Forkwen. The latter got the message and held Tita's attention.

"Well, my son. You are about to take up great responsibilities. We do not expect your mothers or sisters to carry your stool or serve your meals, while our village is the envy of all our neighbours with the many beautiful young girls in almost every compound."

Forkwen broke off and wetted his lips.

"Remember, the first must be from our land," Forkon added.

All the eyes in the room were on the young man. He turned his eyes to the floor. From the smile that played on his face, it was plain that he understood what was being requested of him.

"Is it the right point we are making?" Forkon asked, his eyes searching all the faces.

"Yaah! Very right," the others agreed in unison.

"When next we meet here, my son, we will be expecting you to tell us the name of the young woman who will have the honour to be your first wife. We are sorry that things have to be done with some abruptness. But you understand that we must make up for your absence."

Forkon paused, wetted his lips from his horn, and turned to Abanda. "I guess we should proceed to the next point on our agenda tonight."

Abanda rubbed his palms together. "Great sons of Ngwokwong. Most of us here know the proceedings. However, I must say that a lot of commitment and purpose shall be called for from each and every one of us."

"Ha! Listening to you gives the impression that we are getting ready for a battle," Njang remarked as he moved round to fill the horns of the men in the room.

"Yes, my brothers. This is a battle, in a way," Abanda stressed. "One in which no blood is shared. However, it's one that will draw much sweat from our bodies. If it's not properly planned and executed, Ngwokwong could be a laughingstock for a long time."

He wetted his lips and then went on. "The *kwem* dance we shall perform must be the talk in all homes for a long time to come. We must surpass ourselves. All our jujus must come out in their full splendour. You all will agree with me that Forkon, Chick, and Forkwen have yet to meet their match on the drums?"

A general wave of approval swept through the room as the men grunted their approval.

"The question, my friends, is, who are those to be the mask bearers – in particular, the gorilla skull?" Abanda turned his head, waiting for the others to react.

"Why? You are the right man to wear the gorilla mask." Forkwen looked round for confirmation. The men were all nodding their approval when Abanda intervened.

"No, my brothers, you all know that gone are the days when I used to dance from dawn to dusk without any signs of fatigue. If I am to wear any mask, it must be the cow's skull. If the ground must tremble under our feet on ko'o, as we intend it to, then we must look for a younger man who will ably combine strength, agility, and endurance. Any suggestions?"

"I think Andang is the right person for that." Njang seemed convinced by his own words.

"You all know that Andang is the specialist with the leopard mask. Who would replace him should he bear the gorilla's?" Fomujang wondered aloud.

The others bowed their heads in thought. A name dropped unto Abanda's mind, and his face broke into a broad smile. "Akatcho!" he voiced it out.

"Ah ha! you got it right." Forkwen was almost rising from his seat. "Why did I not think immediately of that young man? He was sensational during the kwem dance that marked the fifth year of reign of the Fon of Etwii."

There was a unanimous "yaah" in the room. The men smiled at each other as if the answer to a puzzle had just been found. Fomujang noted with inward joy and pride how his son's name brought assurance and happiness. His face remained impassive, though.

When the noise that Akatcho's name had generated subsided, Abanda spoke again. "We all know that Azoh is master with the eagle head." Again there was general approval.

"We can move on now to our white blood. Each man must be ready with a full jug. It is true that our neighbours shall not come empty-handed. Yet we must provide in excess. Our honour and generosity must be upheld." Abanda stopped as Forkon attracted his attention.

"It must be said of us that Ngwokwong knows how to prepare for the return of its fon. Remember that our fathers of old maintained that the greatness of the fon when he returns depends on how the people prepare for his return."

Forkon signalled Abanda to carry on. "As for food," Abanda continued, "each woman will cook a full basket of yams and vegetables. Our daughters will prepare the traditional plantain porridge. To do this easily, they will have to meet here on ko'o morning."

By the time the meeting ended, the pot of wine at the centre of the hall was empty. Each man went back to his own end to make known to the people the council's decisions about the forthcoming events.

Chapter 8

After his return from Zang, Akatcho promised himself to go again to Tifang's compound before ko'o market day. He realised his thoughts turned to Nande most of the time. He reminded himself that his mother and sister knew nothing yet about what was going on. His father, he told himself, would decide to inform them at his own chosen moment.

This morning Akatcho realised with mixed feelings that his intended trip to Zang was compromised. His father had informed him the day before of the decision of the village council. The fact that the elders had chosen him to wear the special mask gave him a special feeling of pride. As the hours dragged by, his thoughts kept darting back to Zang. Then it suddenly dawned on him that if he could share his secret with someone, his nerves might relax more readily. Gyam was not around to talk with. His father had left early to meet the other elders at tawh. Languidly Akatcho pulled himself from the flat stone on which he had been lying and walked into the house. He came in as Tengu was lifting the pot from the fire. Muyang was sitting on a mat, painfully trying to undo her plaited hair. He sat on the bamboo bed and folded himself up. He stretched out his legs and began to play absentmindedly with the little stool before him. Slowly, his mind moved back into dreamland. Then his legs stayed still, and his eyes closed.

Tengu had looked up at her son twice, and her motherly instincts told her that the young man's mind was full. She gently pushed a bowl of hot porridge cocoyam towards him. He did not move. She coughed deliberately, and Akatcho started as he came round to the present. His right leg kicked the bowl and almost overturned it. He looked confused but soon picked himself up. He thought for a moment to share with his mother the secret his father had told him. However, his father had warned him to keep it a secret. Fomujang had explained that the mask bearer was not to be known by anyone but the elders. Otherwise, he had warned, the spirits of the land would express their anger.

He looked at the bowl, picked out a piece of cocoyam, and began eating without much appetite. Tengu noticed it immediately.

"You do not look very well, my son. What is the matter?" Tengu looked worried.

"Mother, I am just feeling a little pain in my head."

Tengu did not press him further. She knew that Akatcho would not talk if he did not feel like doing so of his own free accord. Muyang looked at her brother from the corner of her eyes and just managed to keep her mouth closed. She sensed he was troubled. If he did not want to share what was on his mind, it was not her fault anyway. She quietly went on with her hair.

As he made up his mind to visit Sango, Akatcho's appetite improved, and he ate faster. He finished his food and accepted the cup of water from his mother. Then he stood up.

"Mother, I am going to visit my friend."

Muyang looked up at her brother with a sneering smile. "Your friend? Which one? You mean the one in Zang?" Muyang chuckled. She had noticed the suppressed excitement in him since his return from Zang.

"Do not force words out of your brother," Tengu reproached Muyang. "You are going to Sango, my son?"

"Yes, Mother. I need to talk with him." He was already at the door.

Mother and daughter exchanged looks. "I don't mean to hurt you, my daughter," Tengu said cautiously, "but have you done or said anything that could have annoyed your brother?"

"Why would I do something to annoy my brother?" Muyang stopped struggling with her hair.

Tengu explained her worry. "I cannot understand his attitude of a few moments ago, my child. Your brother was only physically present. His mind was elsewhere."

"There is only one explanation, Mother." Muyang beamed mischievously.

Tengu looked steadily at her daughter, with patient expectation. The girl held her mother's eyes for a moment and then started swaying her head from side to side, a crafty smile lingering on her mouth.

"They returned from Zang a couple of weeks ago, remember? Since then my brother has been trying to conceal something. I can feel it. He does not want to answer my questions. All he keeps saying is 'You will soon know'. I have the feeling that something has caught his interest in Zang." She clapped her hands and upturned her palms.

"Maybe, Mother, you know why they went to Zang the other day?"

Tengu did not respond immediately. Her mind was wandering.

"Do you know something, Mother?" Muyang insisted. "I know no one will allow me to go where I want and when I want. But I can sense it … I can feel it. My brother has met a girl."

Her expression had changed to one of irritation and disappointment. Tengu saw the signs immediately and reacted quickly.

"Do not talk like that, my daughter. I think your brother will tell us what is biting him when he comes back." She tried to change the subject. "Aboh, what do you think about your father's proposal yesterday?"

"What proposal? Ah! You mean going to meet my age group in tawh?"

"You will cook well. Will you not?"

The girl did not answer. She loosened the last strand of hair and carried her stool to her mother's side. She sat down and rested her head on Tengu's lap.

"Mother, have you seen the man father was talking about the other day?"

"You mean Tita? No, my little mother. According to your father, he should be slightly shorter and fatter than your brother."

There was a short pause. The girl asked distractedly, "Do you think he can beat my brother?"

"Why should he even want to fight in the first place?" Tengu did not like the question. "Don't think so wildly, my child."

"It just came into my head that … that—" She stopped as the room darkened. Gyam walked in, dragging a jug behind him. He threw himself on a stool and sighed heavily.

"Some of these ceremonies are good. To meet you at home at this time is a blessing, indeed. My stomach has been grumbling like thunder itself."

Muyang raised her head from her mother's lap and smiled as Gyam rubbed his belly. He grinned at her.

"Aboh, have you prepared the little basket you will take tomorrow to tawh? I can see that you will teach your friends how to cook. It cannot be otherwise, seeing that your mother here is the best in this village. Ha ha!"

Tengu pushed a bowl of hot plantain porridge over to Gyam.

"Where is Fomujang?" Gyam became serious.

"He is still away tending to his *Raffia* palms. He is unusually long, though."

Gyam poured himself some wine from the jug.

"You are reducing the wine meant for tomorrow," Tengu said reproachfully.

"I tell you one thing." Gyam drank half the contents of his horn before adding, "Tomorrow, men will leave their intestines behind so as to have real wells that will not fill up fast. If I don't take my share now, I am not sure of being able to taste it tomorrow."

Footsteps sounded at the door. Fomujang crossed the threshold, lowering the calabash from his shoulder. Gyam jumped to his feet and stretched his hands to help.

"Let me help you. How heavy this white blood must be." He carried the jug to the back of the room.

Tengu pushed a stool towards her husband. "You were rather long today. We were beginning to—"

"You remind me," Gyam interrupted her. "I was telling Tengu that you did not stop at a woman's place to fill your stomach." He moved over to his stool and sat down.

"Anyway, I know you have stopped at a certain woman's home." Gyam raised his horn to his mouth and covered the mischievous smile that was threatening to break into a laugh as the others raised eyebrows. Tengu's mouth slowly opened and began to curl into a quiet snarl.

Gyam saw the storm gathering. He knew he could stop it before it exploded.

"And that woman, I tell you, is the best in Ngwokwong." He turned and beamed at Muyang. "Who do you think she would be if her name is not Tengu?"

The sigh that escaped Tengu's mouth betrayed her relief. Muyang looked up at her mother and was amused to see two drops of sweat on her temple. A short silence followed, as each one groped for the right words.

"Where is Akatcho?" Fomujang asked as he settled to enjoy the food Tengu had placed before him.

"Chaah!" Gyam almost rose from his stool. "Will the gods forgive me! I did not even ask after my boy. Where is he?"

"Your son appeared distressed earlier this morning. He refused to say what was eating up his mind. He should be with Sango now." Tengu's voice had grown calm.

Fomujang filled his horn and began eating. Gyam knew of the boy's intended trip to Zang. If he had not gone, then something must have happened to distract him. Whatever it was, he could not ask at that moment, for as elders put it, there was smoke in the house.

"I hope he will be back soon. He has to be at tawh this evening for certain formalities." Fomujang spoke without raising his head from his bowl. He licked his five fingers noisily. Tengu smiled with satisfaction. That was her husband's sign that he enjoyed the food.

Gyam coughed dryly. Fomujang knew the signal. He raised his head, and their eyes met. Gyam raised his brows.

"Well, this morning I told him to remain at home because, as I have already said, he has an important role to play tomorrow."

He looked at his daughter. "You know you will be joining your mates tomorrow?"

"Yes, Father, you told me so yesterday."

"When did he say he would be back?" Gyam asked.

"He did not tell us when. He only—" Muyang stopped. The corner of her eye had caught a slight movement at the door.

"I am back now." Akatcho moved into the room.

"We did not hear you come. You are more noiseless than a cat in your walk." Gyam looked keenly at the boy's face.

Akatcho moved over and sat near his father. He picked out a large piece of cocoyam from the bowl and began to eat. Tengu noticed that the boy looked happier than when he had left.

"You look happier now, my son. One would think that you do not like being alone with your sister and me. I cannot interpret your behaviour this morning otherwise."

"No. Not like that, Mother. I told you I had a headache. It is getting better now."

The woman clapped her hands. "Normally when one gets a headache, one lies down in a cool shed. But you seemed to have calmed yours by moving in the heat out there. That is a miracle."

Fomujang's concern was elsewhere. "This evening, you will go to tawh and make Tita's acquaintance. You will also prepare yourself for tomorrow's ceremony."

The young man looked up at his father. "Father, why was I chosen to—"

"Why do you ask now?" Fomujang cut in sharply. "You will know when the time comes."

Tengu wanted to ask what they were talking about, but the look on her husband's face dissuaded her.

Gyam rose and filled Akatcho's cup.

"Drink some of this, my child. I know it will give you enough energy against tomorrow."

"I think I should be going to tawh now." Akatcho wiped his right palm on his legs.

Fomujang looked outside and noted that the shadows of plants had grown quite long. His eyes held the boy's for a brief moment. "I am counting on you."

Akatcho nodded and moved to the door.

"Did you see Sango?" Tengu asked.

"Yes, Mother." He did not turn.

"How is his mother?"

"Well."

He stepped out and noiselessly walked away. Gyam tilted his head sideways, expecting to hear the fading footsteps.

"He is a cat, that son of yours," Gyam said, looking at Tengu and shaking his head in admiration.

"He is coming back." Muyang's ear had caught some sound of movement outside. They all listened for a while. Gyam shook his head firmly.

"Akatcho does not drag his legs on the ground like that."

Lamu stood in the doorway.

"On an ordinary day, I should be too early." He crossed the threshold, and Fomujang pushed a stool over to him.

"Where is your horn? You announced your tiredness by the way you dragged your feet." Gyam spoke as he poured more wine into his own horn.

"You have heard of the events to take place tomorrow?" Fomujang asked the newcomer.

"Kai! How things happen these days. How is the new fon?"

Fomujang avoided the question. "I hope you and your brothers will join us in tawh tomorrow." Then he quickly briefed Lamu of the plans for the next day.

After a moment's silence, Lamu raised his head from his horn. "I shall leave now. I will go to inform Ahmadou and Baaba so that we can work out our own contribution." There was a look of discomfort on his face.

Fomujang understood what was going on in Lamu's mind. If Tita were to prove the opposite of their expectations, the opposite of his father, as many elders in Ngwokwong feared, then the three *Bororo* families could be obliged to leave and settle elsewhere. Lamu was not fortunate to have a son. He was quite an old man now and would not be happy to have to roam about in search of a new settlement.

Fomujang came round from his thoughts and looked up at Lamu, who had stood up.

"I understand your feelings. We are in no better state of minds ourselves. We all still have to discover him." He paused before asking, "You know what our fathers used to say?"

"What did they say?" Lamu was always amused with the proverbs of the land.

"A bird that is very unsteady on the branch easily reveals its position in a tree. I will advise that you stay calm and let the hunter go by without spotting you."

"I hope you are right. We meet tomorrow," Lamu said and stepped outside.

The chirping of the crickets in the bushes and the croaking of the toads in the ponds indicated how fast the night was falling on Ngwokwong.

Chapter 9

The village was alive before dawn. The early morning wind was cold and biting. This did not, unlike on ordinary days, encourage the children to remain in their beds. The younger boys were looking forward to being told to chase and catch the fowl their fathers would indicate to them. By the second crowing of a cock, the young girls were urged from their homes to move to tawh and start preparations for the day's cooking. As they walked along the paths leading to tawh, they could hear the singing of birds and the rustling of the leaves of plants in the early morning breeze.

Three solitary figures walked up a winding path that led onto a much wider one. They walked with obvious care, for the day had not broken completely. Ijang led the way. She had gone some distance ahead of the others. She decided to urge her friends to move faster.

"*Uuuhu!* Am I too fast?"

"Do you want to be the first to reach tawh?"

There was a touch of impatience in Nyoh's voice. She was at the rear. Her remarkable bulk did not make walking easy for her. Ijang waited; the others soon caught up with her, and they went on again in a single file.

"Have you met that boy?" Muyang asked to no one in particular.

"What boy?" Ijang stopped and turned round. "You mean Tita? Chaah! Is that how you call him?"

"How do you want me to call him? He is not the fon yet," Muyang argued.

"H'mmm! That one! The way he looked at me yesterday." Ijang clapped her hands as they carried on.

"So, you have met him too?" Muyang asked, surprised.

"I was going my way yesterday when he came out of his mother's hut by chance. You should have seen how he looked at me." Ijang clapped her hands once more in an exaggerated gesture.

"Tell us what happened. How did he look at you?" Nyoh urged her on.

"He just stood there looking at me like a hungry cock looking at corn on a wall." The three girls burst out with laughter.

The day was breaking fast. They could now see clearly around them. They were just a short distance away from their destination. The voices that reached them from tawh informed them that they were not the first to arrive there.

The wide yard spread in front of tawh hall. It had some curious features. The centre was a raised, circular piece of ground, with numerous depressions on its flat top. At one end, a flat, egg-shaped stone seemed to grow out of the ground. It was smooth, slightly tilted backwards, and stood well over a metre above the surface. Forkon surveyed the yard with apparent satisfaction. It was wide enough, he convinced himself. It only needed to be watered and swept to be ready to receive the biggest population Ngwokwong had hosted for a very long time. He then turned to the back of the huts, where the young men were busy slaughtering and chopping fowls, pigs and goats. He encouraged them with a few words. Then he moved from hut to hut, greeting and encouraging the young girls and women involved with the cooking.

In one of the inner rooms of tawh, three men sat talking together.

"We are telling you all these, my son, for your good and that of your people. We do not doubt that you will rule your people well. Yet you must be guided. Our fathers before us maintained that no man grows before he is born."

Abanda paused to see if the young man was following him.

"Have you practised the speech we taught you last evening, my son?"

"Yes. Shall I repeat it to your hearing?"

The two elderly men nodded, and Tita spoke for a while.

"We are glad that you can remember every word. You are young and not experienced in the art of talking to a crowd. Yet you must talk to your people as a father to his children. You should speak calmly, clearly, and with dignity. Do you understand, my son?"

While Forkon spoke, Tita looked at the ground. When he stopped, the young man looked up, and their eyes met. Tita quickly dropped his. Forkon noticed the boy's nervousness. Well, he is still growing up, he consoled himself.

"I think it would be a good thing for you to go round and encourage your people as they make preparations for the day's activities."

Tita stood up and moved out of the room.

"I hope he grows fast," Abanda remarked. "Has Fomujang arrived yet?

"Yaah! He is receiving and arranging the jugs of wine. Azoh and his friends are oiling their masks." A thought seemed to drop into his mind. "Do you think that young man will carry the gorilla mask well?"

"Have no doubts," Abanda beamed. "If there is one person in Ngwokwong today capable of creating sensation with the gorilla mask, he is the one."

He added as if to someone invisible in the room, "Today will be remembered and will stay in the memory of men for a very long time."

There were altogether seven huts for Tita to visit. He decided to start with the one on the left side of tawh yard. In that hut, Muyang and Ijang were peeling the plantains while Nyoh washed the intestines of a goat. A huge pot rested on three stones in the centre of the hut. The wood burning beneath it was glowing red-hot. The girls were working fast. They intended to finish quickly in order to have enough time to make themselves beautiful for the day's events. They knew all the young men from villages beyond would turn up and with specific interests.

When there remained only a few plantains, Muyang pulled the basket of bitterleaf vegetables to her side. "Join me after you have put the plantains into the pot." She started to separate the leaves from the stems.

Ijang asked, with no apparent interest, "Where is your brother? Akatcho is invisible these days."

Muyang threw a sidelong glance at her friend. She was aware that her friend was attracted to her brother. It was too early to hurt her friend's feelings with what she secretly believed pulled her brother's attention to Zang.

"I don't know what is troubling him. Yesterday he complained of headache."

Muyang's hesitation did not escape Ijang. She thought Muyang had not really answered her question. She wanted to press further, but at that moment the room darkened.

Tita stepped in. "The day has broken, girls?" He put on a smile.

Ijang recovered first. "Yes, it has broken." Her voice quivered slightly.

"I was passing and heard your voices. I came in to greet you."

"That is kind of you," Ijang responded

Tita looked down at Muyang. The girl looked up at the same time, and their eyes locked. The young man's heart jolted within him. His eyes refused to blink, though the smoke in the room was hurting them. For a fraction of a second, his body shivered perceptibly. His lips parted, but no sound came out. He stood like a rock.

"Will you be with us longer this time around?" Ijang's voice came from a distance.

The young man started and struggled within himself to regain control of his racing heart. "What did you say?"

Ijang repeated her question. He just nodded and managed to pull his eyes away from Muyang's.

"I would like to eat the plantains you are cooking." Though he looked at the pot on the fire, he somehow saw only the face he just forced his eyes from.

"We are flattered," Ijang said, trying to make sense of the tense atmosphere.

Tita nodded again and dragged one leg after the other away from the room. As his footsteps died away, Ijang burst out excitedly, "You understand now, don't you?"

"Understand what?" Muyang's voice was snappy.

Ijang was surprised to note that her friend sounded irritated.

"I mean he looked at you the same way he looked at me yesterday."

"What is that supposed to mean? Why look at people as if they were apparitions?"

"Don't you see that he likes you? He did not as much as notice my presence." Nyoh twisted her lips in a gesture that betrayed her envy.

Ijang felt the tension gathering.

"If we continue talking, we will be the last to finish cooking."

An uneasy silence fell in the room as each girl wrestled with her thoughts.

Chapter 10

The yard became smaller and smaller as more and more people came into Ngwokwong from beyond the hills. The young and the old, the weak and the strong were all turning up. No one was willing to stay back and only be told of the events of this day. Women and children squatted on the soft grass around the yard, occupying one full flank. The men sat opposite to the women and children.

The old people around could only compare the turnout to the one that had marked the passing away of the grandfather of the present fon of Etwii. A few of them present were recounting the events of that remarkable event. Groups formed around those who could remember and recount the tale. The thickest one encircled Amuteng, who had come all the way from Tugi. She was a woman of advanced age. Her eyes still shone with a light that pulled people to her side. Her thin arms were still strong enough to execute exact gestures.

"Eeeeh chaah." Amuteng's arms bent at the elbows and shot upwards, and her fingers spread out. "I am telling you just as it happened. I was only a little girl then. I can still see it in my mind as though it were happening now. There were all sorts of jujus. But I could not dare to look at the gorilla head when it appeared last of all."

"The gorilla head – or mask?" the women around her asked with one voice.

"Yes, my children. A real skull of a gorilla head only appears on unique occasions that involve all our villages. It is the father of all other jujus, which we see often. As I was saying—"

"Who carried it?" a woman asked.

"Does a woman know who carries what juju?

The old woman asked but did not expect or wait for an answer.

"Aha! I forgot to tell you that the father of the present fon of Etwii was crowned that very day."

"Is that what will happen today?" another woman asked.

"How would I know?"

The old woman went on, but her tone was more irritated.

"That is the curse on us women. We do not know what our men are planning. We just see things happen, and we cannot even question." The old woman paused and shook her head sadly.

Another woman spoke. "But I remember that no such occasion took place when the Fon of Etwii disappeared. I mean, the father of the present fon. Why was that so?"

"Those are not things for us to discuss, my child. But I can tell you this. Our ancestors maintained that the greatest abomination in any man's life is for him to take his own life. Should that happen, such a man is asking to be wiped out of the memory of men. We need not talk about it, my children, at the risk of going against the laws of our land. That is what happened."

"But why would a fon commit suicide?" a man persisted. "I never heard of such an abomination."

"Chaah! Not the fon," Amuteng whispered. "It was a *Bororo* man who hanged himself in one of the fon's farmlands. He was—"

The old woman ceased her whispering as the noise of the drumming filled the air. The fons moved in a single file. Ahead of the long procession was the Fon of Zang. His long robe of red and green stretched right down to his ankles. A similarly coloured cap covered his head, a red feather sticking out at the side. His staff hit the ground at regular intervals as he walked with slow, deliberate steps. He stared ahead of him as he turned over many thoughts in his mind. He would not have to speak for long, but the little he would say must carry the weight of the day.

The Fon of Guneku returns (2015)

Behind him came the Fon of Tugi. His robe was of green and brown, while his cap was of red and brown. His staff, with its curious designs, made no sound as it touched the ground. Unlike the thoughtful figure in front of him, he was turning his head from side to side, taking in with admiration the size of the crowd. Twice he adjusted the red feather on the left side of his cap.

The Fon of Etwii came next. He was dressed like the Fon of Zang except for his cap, which was the fibrous black one, with its very noticeable bright-red feather. His brows were gathered, and the muscles of his face tightened as he remembered his father. Nothing of this nature had taken place. The council of elders of Etwii had decided against any lavish ceremony to mark the return of their departed fon. It was an abomination for a man to take his own life. No reason was good enough to oblige a real man to take his own life. A stranger to Etwii had defiled the land and angered their ancestors by taking his own life on the farmland that belonged to the fon. It would take seven years to cleanse the land and appease the ancestors before the fon's return could properly be celebrated. The young fon shook his head sadly as he resigned himself to the fact that he still had to wait another two years before organising the grand ceremony that would give him the full authority in his role. His pace had slowed down as his mind wandered in the past. Tita coughed dryly behind him. He came back to the present and realised that he had dropped some steps behind. He quickly covered the space. Tita caught up with him. Forkon and those following did the same.

Forkon looked for the fifth time at Tita's outfit before him. He hoped the loin was well chosen. Again, he considered the black cap from which no feather stuck yet, the beads around his neck, and his black loin interwoven with white and red strips covering from the waist to his ankles. The young man's torso was bare. His muscles bulged and many were the young men and women that noted that with admiration. He swung his hands freely by his sides. His eyes searched through the section of the yard occupied by the women. Where was that face that had quickened his heartbeat that morning? He looked so hard and long that his eyes hurt.

The strain in his eyes began to tell; they watered, and he dropped his head. He raised the fingers of his left hand and pressed them against his eyes to clear his vision. He continued moving. When he raised his head, he came to an abrupt stop. Those ahead had come to a standstill.

The noise of the crowd had decreased to whispers. The people just stared at the long file of dignitaries. The Fon of Zang moved to the flat, vertical egg-shaped stone. His stool was placed at its foot. He sat down and leaned backwards, resting against the stone. The Fon of Tugi sat to his right, while the Fon of Etwii sat to the left. Tita, closely followed by Forkon, sat to the right of the Fon of Tugi. It took a while for all the men to find seats for themselves. The drummers who brought up the rear carried their instruments to the raised piece of ground at the centre of the yard. They carefully placed their drums into depressions that had been prepared to hold them in position.

Then silence dropped onto Ngwokwong. Even the animals appeared hit by a spell. Only the splattering of the stream defied the silence. After a while, Forkon rose and walked to the centre of the yard. He meandered among the drummers to the huge ngom and picked up the two stout sticks by its side. He contemplated the drum. Large scars showed on its sides. The two elliptical openings at the top that narrowed to a small slit at the middle had grown wider. For a split second, he recalled the last time this drum had been beaten. He had been a very young man then, and no one could have convinced him then that he would one day take a turn in calling up the ancestors of the land with the language of the ngom.

Slowly, his eyes wandered round the multitude and finally settled on the Fon of Zang, who gave a quick nod. He pulled a stool towards him and sat down. He raised the two sticks and held them horizontally across the drum. His hands stayed there for a while. Then, without warning, Abanda jumped from his seat and walked briskly round the space between the drummers and the crowd. He made three swift rounds, and each time he passed by the fons, he let out a mighty shout – the war cry of the people. In the middle of each shout, he called out the name of the late fon. He passed the fons for the third time and stood to let out his war cry: *"Waa-hoo – Azah – uuh-yaaah!"*

As the shout ended, Forkon heaved a sigh and brought down the sticks on the drum with such a mighty force that the earth beneath the people

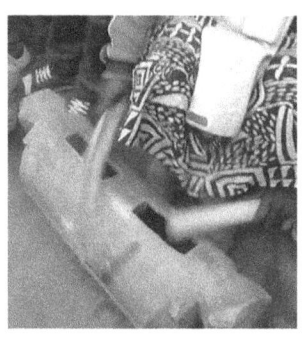

trembled. Most of the women and children started out of their seats, such was the abruptness and loudness of the drum. For a while, most of the people pressed their palms against their ears. The drumming went on for some time and then stopped as suddenly as it had begun. Forkon rose and made his way back to his former seat. Things had started so abruptly that the women were holding tightly to their breasts so as not to betray the beating of their hearts. The little children who a while ago had been playing cheerily about were now clinging to their mothers.

The Fon of Zang waited a while; then he rose to his full height, and his eyes swept through the crowd. His huge personality commanded silence. He moved a step ahead, and his right hand went to his head to adjust his cap. As he moved back his hand, his right thumb accidentally pushed the red feather off his cap. The feather did not fall straight to the ground. Instead, it floated in the  air. It seemed to dance at the same distance above the ground. The crowd gasped. The men, nearer the scene, blinked faster to clear the mist from their eyes. The fon just stood and stared. He held himself together with an effort. He was just going to put out his hand and catch the feather, when it floated away to his right. The fon's *chinda*, who was standing behind him, made to go after it, but the fon instinctively laid a restraining hand on him. He was calmer now, and he watched in silence and with interest. The breeze was very weak, but the feather danced on, maintaining its height above ground level. A few men and a good number of women were already on their feet, preparing to take to their heels. However, the curiosity to witness more and the doubt as to the reality of the event held them back.

Forkon was dazed. He wiped his eyes and opened them wider. Tita saw the feather approach him. He lifted his buttocks above his stool, and he only stood his ground because he did not want to be the first to start running away. Very slowly, the feather drifted past the Fon of Tugi, who just sat in a helpless heap, his eyes threatening to leave their sockets. The young Fon of Etwii just hid his face in his hands and did not see the feather move towards Tita. When it was just above Tita's head, it seemed to lose its floating power, and it fell at his feet. He leaped from his seat, completely overtaken by fear. He was picking up his shivering body when a powerful voice spoke. "Sit down, my son, and fear not, for your father has spoken from beyond."

All eyes turned towards the Fon of Zang, the only man who appeared to have kept his calm. If those near him could have listened closely, they would have heard the gnashing of his teeth. That meant he was trying to bring himself back to his normal state. Though the curious happening was excitingly frightful to the older ones present, the children were smiling and attracted by it. The little children had watched the feather with ecstasy and interest. Only the grim and terrified looks of their mothers had stopped them from shouting out with joy.

Two long steps took the Fon of Zang to Tita's side. He calmly led the young man back to his seat. He picked up the feather and stuck it into

Tita's cap. Then he returned to his original position. He raised his head and looked at the gigantic rock - kob Azah - at the summit of the hill.

"Fathers of Ngwokwong, your sons and daughters have come from far and near to pay their homage and respect. We call on you for protection against any evil spirit that may roam about around us. May you show us your approval that your message a few moments ago was well understood."

The fon lowered his head and looked round. His hands spread out. "My beloved children assembled here today," – he brought his hands together in a gathering gesture – "we are all witnesses to something that we have never heard of occurring in similar gatherings in the past." He raised his brows enquiringly at the other two fons.

"Never!" the Fon of Tugi confirmed, still gripping his staff to steady himself.

"What an event!" The young Fon of Etwii was still visibly shaken.

"Yes, I was as astonished and shaken as you all were," the Fon of Zang went on.

The murmur that rose from the crowd interrupted him. The people looked suspiciously around. Children pointed up at Kob Azah, where clouds circled its topmost part. A human figure holding a staff appeared to emerge from the  rock. It stood there for a few moments and then was swallowed by the clouds. Each man and woman present experienced a number of emotions.

But fear and curiosity stood out as the most noticeable. Could there be an invisible being amongst them? Their eyes asked what their mouths could not put into words.

The fons of Tugi and Etwii rose from their stools and stood beside the Fon of Zang. They, too, had seen the apparition. One would have expected real panic to seize the crowd, but it was the opposite from the incident with the floating feather. Fear quickly gave way to whispered questions. The most entertained were the children, who were all raising their voices in excitement. For some long moments, no one was sure what was going to happen next.

The Fon of Zang coughed dryly, and the crowd went expectantly silent. His opened palms shot upwards. "Was there ever a people that courageously faced adversity when its leader quailed from it? No, my people, no leader is worth the title if he cannot face adversity." He paused and brought his hands together, each palm clasping the other

"Whatever the case, we must admit that our ancestors are talking to us in their own peculiar way. They are glad that our son here is going to shoulder the responsibilities that his father left. Though I must tell you, it will not be today that Tita will take up his traditional responsibilities. He first has to get acquainted with all our laws and sacred ways before he is crowned." He turned and faced the young man. The latter had not yet regained his self-control.

"Oh, chosen son of his fathers, we cannot go on until you let your children know your mind and will. We must know if you are willing to keep onto the path of light which your father before you for many years maintained."

107

The fon sat down and wiped the perspiration from his face with his palm. The sun's burning intensity had lessened. Tita was sweating freely. The drops of sweat ran down his face and dropped onto his robe. Forkon whispered in his ear, and he stood up. He spoke quickly, his voice trembling slightly. It was, however, loud enough for all to hear.

"My fathers; my mothers; children of Ngwokwong, Zang, Tugi and Etwii – I salute you all. I, your son, am willing to lead my people through mist, rain, heat, and any obstacle that may stand between us and the path of light."

The crowd burst into cheers. The people shouted out encouraging words to Tita. He waited for the noise to die down. Forkon whispered something in his ear. When Tita resumed his speech, his eyes shone with confidence.

"My dear fathers, mothers, brothers, and sisters, here I am as your son. Nothing else but your son and child. I am no god, but just a child like any other." He paused as Forkon touched him with his elbow.

A shocked murmur went through the crowd. Forkon, from the corner of his eye, saw the bewildered expression on the faces of the fons. They were exchanging looks blankly. Was Tita denying his responsibility? It had never been heard of!!

Forkon smiled with inward satisfaction. The desired effect of those words was being achieved. A good leader, Forkon believed, should be able to arouse anxiety and create suspense. He touched Tita again, and the latter went on with his speech.

"Oh, my dear people, didn't our fathers of old maintain that children are taught so that they may teach their fathers? Who is it that teaches the children? Yes, dear people, a father teaches the child, and the child in turn uses that knowledge to teach the father and also the mother."

The applause that saluted the words was deafening. He waited for the noise to die down.

"I, Tita, am your son. I am willing and ready to drink from your cup of wisdom. And I promise before the gods and our ancestors to use that very wisdom to keep you, all of you, in the path of light."

The last words were drowned as the drums sounded furiously. Tita's mother ran to her son's side and fell on her knees. She caught her son's feet and fondled them with motherly warmth. She clapped and danced, and her tears flowed freely. A few other women joined her.

Most of the elders of Ngwokwong were smiling with relief. Who would have believed that Tita, after his long and repeated absences, could stand before such a huge crowd and speak so clearly and sensibly? The ceremony decidedly was going to be one of extraordinary events. First the floating feather and the human form up on the kob. Then the unexpected skill of the young man who might, after all, return as a greater fon than expected. When at last silence returned, the Fon of Zang rose, and his eyes swept across the multitude.

"Could he have spoken greater words? Many are our children who thirst for the wisdom of the elders, yet few are those who truly drink from the cup of wisdom." The fon's smile broadened as he turned his eyes on Tita.

"You are already proving to us all that you are the true son of your father. Indeed, you already speak like the father of your people. I, fon Teghenicha, speaking on behalf of all the fons of all the villages that make up our clan, am now asking you to keep your promise, and your father, as well as those who journeyed long before him, will shower you with their favours."

The fon turned and stepped forward; his eyes flashed and his nostrils widened. His right fist formed and shot forward as he roared, "Let the great dance begin!"

Chapter 11

Forkon stepped up to the ngom for the second time and shared a few words with the drummers. Akuro, whose drum was as big as the ngom, though it had a different sound, sat to his right. Forkwen stood to the left, his legs straddled to hold his drum steady. The bottom of his drum had a wide circular opening, while the top was covered with a tough cow skin. Chick sat on two such smaller drums, passed his hands under his legs, and waited with anticipation. Already his mouth hung open, his tongue sticking out to one side.

Forkon gave the first notes on the ngom, and the others joined in. The music went on for a while, and the crowd was beginning to sway to the rhythm, when it suddenly stopped. Forkon jumped to his feet, and his voice rang out loud and clear as he released the first notes of the kwem dance. His voice trembled with suppressed excitement.

"Oh Mutachibi, oh Mutachibi, oh Mutachibi." He raised his right fist and shook it proudly in the air. *"Ta-ta-ta-ta – chibi!"* he thundered.

"Yaah!" the crowd roared in answer.

"Chibi!"

"Yaah!"

Then there was silence as he sat back on his stool. He looked up and saw Abanda coming from behind the hut.

He picked up his sticks and made a sign to his friends, and the drums cried out in a deafening excitement. The dancers next appeared. They came out from one of the huts in a long file and started doing a stooping dance round the space between the crowd and the drummers. They were bare-bodied except for the loincloths around their waists. In their right hands they brandished unsharpened machetes. Their scabbards hung from ropes made of cloth, which were passed across their right shoulders to their left sides. They were mostly young and middle-aged men. As they danced on, their voices were raised to the sky with shouts and exclamations of excitement.

Sango danced with a grace that caught most eyes. He left his position and ran round in the circle of dancers. He stooped at short regular intervals, and each time he did so he scraped or cut the ground with his machete. At each stroke of the machete, the dancers flew into the air, swung round, and danced with a greater determination to surpass themselves.

Abanda walked into the circle of dancers. He took the machete from one of the dancers and moved furtively around. Then he burst into short runs that soon changed into long, sophisticated steps. He came round to where Sango danced and raised his machete above his head. The younger man did the same, and the sharp sound that was produced as the metals clashed in mid-air sent a cold shiver up the women's spines. The sparks flew and melted into emptiness. As Abanda went on with his stylish steps round the circle, the atmosphere resonated with the clash of machetes. His voice rose above the noise of the music.

"*Ta-ta-ta-ta – chibi!*" he shouted, his right leg rising and falling back to hit the ground.

"*Yaah!*" came the deafening answer.

"Chibi!"

"Yaah!"

"This is how Ngwokwong celebrates the return of her father!"

Then he went round the circle and stopped in front of Forkon. For a brief moment they exchanged looks. Then his machete rose and cut through the air. The drumming stopped instantly. The crowd clapped and shouted with excitement as the dancers disappeared behind the hut.

When they reappeared, each dancer wore silver beads that hung below the knees. The beads contained pebbles that emitted shrill sounds as they freely rolled and hit the internal walls. Some of the dancers moved into the hall, while the others encircled the drummers. Forkon stood up, and the veins on his neck bulged as he shouted out the notes of the kwem dance. Sango looked expectantly towards the hall. Fomujang's head came round the door, and he nodded significantly. Sango ran round the circle three times, and when he came to his original position, he cut the air three times with his machete. He leapt into the air, and as his feet touched the ground, all the drums cried out in unison. The dancers spread out in a wider circle and danced with renewed vitality.

Fomujang emerged from the hall playing a flute. The notes from the flute were solemn. All eyes on the yard turned towards tawh hall. Calmly, the mask bearers emerged and walked in a single file onto the scene of action.

The bearer of the leopard mask drifted on behind Fomujang. The cow and then the eagle mask bearers followed. The noise on tawh yard rose higher as children burst into uncontrollable wailing, frightened by the masks. They clung to their mothers. Those who sat closest to the circle of dancers began to scramble towards the outer circles.

The sun had gone out of sight, but the red glow of its rays still lit the village. The cool breeze that swept across Ngwokwong revitalised the dancers and drummers. The bearer of the leopard mask moved into the circle of dancers. Like the others, he had a brown, fibrous cloth covering his entire body. A broad ring covered with a multicoloured cloth encircled his waist. The cloth extended to the ground, keeping his feet out of sight. Special beads were tied round his ankles. As he moved around, the beads rubbed against each other, sending out uniform music of a different sound and nature than that of the silver beads of the ordinary dancers.

Steadily, the other masks bearers moved into the circle of dancers, turning their masked faces in all directions. The leopard mask created fear even amongst the women. Its gaping mouth, with its teeth-like projections, was more than the children could stand. They hurried behind their mothers and clung tightly to them.

Without warning, the tempo in tawh yard rose suddenly, as the masks bearers suddenly spread out and started dancing. They danced in a seemingly chaotic manner but, surprisingly, keeping to the rhythm of the music. They danced in and out of the circle of dancers. Each time they approached the women, the children cried out helplessly and gripped their mothers more. Many women just buried their faces in their palms when the leopard mask came near.

The kwem dance had been going on for a while, when the Fon of Zang rose from his stool. Sango stepped out of the circle and looked up enquiringly at the fon. The old man nodded, and he darted away towards the little hut. The fons of Etwii and Tugi followed him into the hut. The Fon of Zang moved over to the drummers and winked at Forkon. The latter stood up and smiled his understanding of the fon's signal. He stepped aside, but not before covering his stool with a piece of cloth handed to him by the fon's *chinda*. The fon sat and looked around at the others, his great personality gripping and galvanising the drummers. He rolled up his sleeves and then rose again and let out a thunderous shout. It was loud and strange. Very few present could understand the meaning and implication of it.

Then the gorilla mask appeared. If the leopard mask created fear, this one sent terror up the spines of all the women and children. The women started scrambling to the far ends of the yard. The mask was slowly turned from side to side as its bearer walked, between the two fons, towards the centre of the circle. Its wide, gaping mouth with the uneven set of teeth-like projections was stunningly compelling. Its upper lip, with its long stiff whiskers, was pulled back from the upper "teeth" in a horrendous snarl. The small forehead, with numerous depressions, created a sinister appearance. Yet the elderly ones, who looked on with admiration, considered this mask a symbol of unity and oneness. What brought evil, they usually maintained, was not always that which proclaimed it.

In the circle, the gorilla creature stood before the Fon of Zang. The latter bowed twice. Then Sango detached himself from the circle and went round the mask bearers three times before releasing the well-known notes of the kwem dance.

"Ta-ta-ta-ta – chibi!"

"Yaah!" came the deafening response from the crowd.

"Chibi!"

"Yaah!"

"Our ancestors are with us!" the fon concluded at the top of his voice. Without warning, the gorilla mask bearer shot forward. He moved swiftly round, his hands tearing the air before him. Each time he made a complete round, he shouted out the name of one of the four villages. At the pronunciation of the last name, Ngwokwong, he leapt into the air. As he landed, the drummers burst into action. The circle of dancers widened to make more room for the masks bearers. The gorilla mask bearer danced round the other three masks, touching each in turn. As the drumming went into frenzy, he danced in and out of the circle with dazzling dexterity, cutting the air here and stamping the ground there. It was creating sensation, and the crowd cheered with approval.

Abanda smiled with satisfaction under his mask. He was proud to have made the right choice. He so admired the gorilla mask bearer's performance that he almost slowed down his own pace. He quickly recovered as Chick's drum cried louder. The drummer's fingers threatened to burst the drum he played. Sweat flowed freely down his face and dripped onto his hanging tongue, but he seemed oblivious of that. The veins on his hands and neck stood out, stretched to the limit. The Fon of Zang shoved his cap to the back of his head. The tempo had risen to fever height, and his head shot from side to side as he shouted out the notes of the dance to the others. He was an expert on the huge ngom, and he showed it.

The number of people dancing increased. Only the sick and very old could resist joining the dancing crowd. Three outer circles quickly formed, the women forming the outermost one. The crowd so thickened around the dancers that the latter could not freely swing their machetes without the risk of hurting each other. Most dancers had slipped their machetes into their scabbards, while some others just held theirs steadily before them.

The glow from the sun's rays had completely disappeared. At a certain instant, the Fon of Zang raised his right hand. The gorilla mask bearer danced like one moving on springs. His performance was electrifying, and the crowd went wild. The dance went on with no sign of stopping. Then, suddenly, he danced out of the circle and stopped abruptly. With gestures, he urged the other mask bearers to line up behind him. Sango led them back into the hut. Not long after that, Forkon replaced the Fon of Zang, who then regained his place beside the other two fons.

As the intensity of the dance gradually reduced, Tita's mother rose from where she had been sitting. White beads around her head designating her rank. She gestured to a group of young girls to follow her. Muyang was amongst them. Tita almost rose from his seat when he caught sight of her. His eyes followed Muyang until she disappeared into the hut.

A number of young men soon appeared carrying jugs of wine. These they arranged in five rows of ten jugs. The young girls next emerged from various huts with bowls of foods of all types. These they positioned opposite to where the jugs of wine stood before retaking their places on the yard. Some of the young men came out of the hall with huge earthen jars and placed them in the centre of the yard. Abanda whispered something to Akatcho, who sat close to him. The young man got up and moved to the hall. He emerged shortly afterwards, carrying an old *Raffia* bag. He walked over to where Tita was sitting and placed the bag at his feet. Then he walked back to his own seat. The crowd was quiet, and the younger people turned their heads from side to side, wondering what was to follow. Many others were hungry and thirsty, exhausted after the performance of the kwem dance.

Gyam's tongue ran over his lips several times and he painfully swallowed his saliva. Next to him was Mukom, from Tugi. Their conversation had been interrupted when Akatcho had moved towards Tita. Like his friend, Mukom was showing signs of impatience. He pulled his *Raffia* bag from his back and let it dangle between his legs. He peered into it to reassure himself that his horn was in there. He closed his eyes and tried to focus his mind elsewhere. He started when Gyam tapped him on the back.

"I can hear your heart jumping in your chest. I was just wondering who will hold your hand and lead you home after this." Gyam stretched his lips in the direction of the jugs.

"Ha! Do you think I have weak blood like you? I, Mukom, who emptied two full jugs of wine and could still make a difference amongst my five wives?" Mukom hit his chest with pride. He was about to heap more praises on himself for his drinking prowess, when his friend put a finger to his lips.

"Ssssst. The fon is about to speak." Gyam added, almost in a whisper, "But remember that the wine you just alluded to was not from Ngwokwong. Even a newly born baby can empty a jug of Tugi wine and still look up clearly at its mother."

Mukom shifted uneasily on his stool but could not retort because the fon was up and the yard had gone dead silent.

Chapter 12

The Fon of Zang stood looking at the jugs of wine and bowls of food. He nodded his head silently in approbation. It was clear that there was going to be more than enough to drink and eat for everyone. He looked up, and his lips parted.

"Ngwokwong! Oh, worthy children of this land! It is great indeed when the child properly mourns the father." He raised his head, and his eyes focussed on the mighty rock at the summit of the hill. "Father of his people, we ask for your blessings, protection, and guidance."

He lowered his head and turned towards Forkon. The latter rose and picked up the bag at Tita's feet. He straightened and waited. The fon moved to one of the jugs, and Forkon joined him. He put his right hand into the bag and brought out a black arch-shaped horn with various designs all over it. He bent over, filled it with wine, and then turned and stared meaningfully at the other fons. The leaders stood and joined him. Forkon signalled Tita to join the fons. Then the five men moved to the back of the hall.

It was a while before they returned. As the fons moved over to their seats, Forkon walked to the centre of the yard. "Worthy sons and daughters of their father, does a child refuse to eat from the same bowl as its father?" He looked round enquiringly.

"No," and "How can it?" the people answered simultaneously.

"Yes. No child worthy of its father's trust will ignore its father's bowl. Our departed father has tested of this food. Are we his true and faithful children who will not taste of these?"

He spread his ten fingers, pointing at the food and drinks before him. He expected no answer as he moved two steps sideways and stood by the jugs of wine.

"This is what Ngwokwong has prepared to share with its brothers and sisters from far and near who have come to stand by her in these distressing moments. We appreciate the great contribution from our brothers and sisters from Zang, Tugi, Etwii and the *Bororo* community".

He stopped, and Abanda suddenly jumped up. He moved briskly around the jugs of wine and bowls of food. When he came close to the fons, he roared, *"Ta-ta-ta-ta – chibi!"*.

"Yaah!"

"Chibi!"

"Yaah!"

"We must not sleep when great things are at hand!" he *shouted* at the top of his voice.

As Forkon went back to his seat, his eyes searched Akatcho's, and he nodded. The young man stood up, and ten others instantly joined him. They all held small calabashes with holes in the necks. A huge clay pot was placed at the centre of the yard, and five jugs of wine were emptied into it. A large calabash was filled and placed in front of the fons. Forkon stood up and filled the royal horns. The young men filled their calabashes and went round filling the horns of the men and small calabashes of the women. The girls were busy sharing food from the bowls to various groups of men and women. The fons of Zang and Etwii were helping themselves from a large bowl of plantain porridge with visibly large appetites.

The Fon of Tugi quietly sipped from his horn and patiently waited for his special dish. Muyang placed two little bowls before him. She stretched herself and was going to turn round, when Tita's eyes caught hers. He was staring at her, and she stared back.

The fon raised his head and said, "You will bring some water to your father, my child?"

The girl jumped slightly. "Did you speak to me, Father?"

"Yes, my child. I need some water to drink. You see, no wine can replace water."

"Yes, Father." She hurried away, wondering whether the old man had noticed her attitude with Tita.

The fon quietly pulled the bowls closer to him and plunged his hand into the one with the well-rounded cocoyam foofoo. He had not noticed the girl's absentmindedness. He did not even notice that it was a different girl that brought him water. He tossed a huge lump of foofoo into his mouth and sent vegetables after it. He chomped the mixture in his mouth for a while and then swallowed, releasing a snap in his throat. He took the little calabash that was by his side and drank water from it.

The yard was filled with noise and movement. At one corner of the yard, the crowd thickened. In the centre, Gyam and Mukom were engaged in a passionate argument. "The size of your horn just doesn't agree with your belly," Mukom was saying with grimaces.

Gyam held up his horn to his eye and looked it over as if seeing it for the first time. "Are you talking of this or of that pot in your hands?" He called out, "Eh, boys, your father's horn is empty. Would you do something about it?" Gyam was pointing at Mukom's horn.

"One cannot deny the fact that your Ngwokwong wine is good. But—" Mukom stopped to empty his horn. He had spotted the boys coming around with their calabashes.

"Now you are talking like a great son of Tugi who can appreciate quality. Ha ha. Give me your hand for acknowledging a fact at last." Gyam stretched out his hand, but Mukom ignored it.

"If you had let me finish what I was saying, you would not have made such a ridiculous mistake. Take back your hand, else the wind may sever it." Mukom covered his mouth with his horn, satisfied with himself.

"Mistake?" Gyam chuckled, searching the smiling faces surrounding them. "Do I ever make mistakes? Ah, I see that my good friend is just covering up, is it not?" There was much laughter from the onlookers.

"You mean covering up the fact that our wine is better than yours?" Mukom retorted. Again there was much laughter around the two men. Someone choked and coughed noisily nearby.

"Ah ha. You all see what Ngwokwong wine can do to people?" Mukom added.

"I see what you mean. Although you cannot put it rightly. Are you not saying that he is not a good drinker?" Gyam responded, trying to make out who the victim was.

"What a good interpreter you make. You seem to look at things from a woman's perspective. You know that only women make bad drinkers."

"You speak of women as if Tugi can boast of any. Have you not seen the pride of Ngwokwong?" Gyam pointed in the direction of the young girls.

Mukom did not look. Instead, he dipped his hand into the bowl that had been placed before them. He filled his mouth with plantain porridge. Gyam followed his example.

"If you can pass through your door today, then I am not Gyam."

"Are you saying that our women cannot cook as well as this, if not better?"

"As if you have any to be proud of," Gyam spoke as he selected a large plantain from the bowl and placed it between his teeth. He bit deeply, and only a very small piece remained in his hand. His cheeks were so full he could not manage to talk and chew at the same time.

Akatcho and his friends made sure that no horns were left empty. Already forty-two jugs stood empty. Yet those brought by the visitors had not been touched.

The *Bororo* family sat at one corner of the yard. They were quietly eating and drinking, like the others. Amina had joined Muyang's group. The girls admired her long strands of hair as they glided across her back with each head movement. She spoke very little, for she was not fluent with the language.

The cold was coming fast. The chirping of crickets was already announcing the approach of darkness. The serving boys were sweating profusely. Over five jugs still stood untouched. Some people were already spread out on the floor, snoring loudly. Gyam and Mukom talked at the same time without making any sense. As the emptied bowls were taken away from their feet, the fons rubbed their oily palms on their legs. They emptied their cups and stood up one after the other, adjusting their robes around them. They looked around the yard and were not surprised at the number of people stretched out and snoring. The Fon of Zang spoke to those who could still hear and make sense of his words.

"This day, Ngwokwong has proved itself the worthy and true child of its father. We will leave now. We are not by any means calling for an end to this ceremony. Those who cannot go back this evening to their homes may stay in Ngwokwong until tomorrow. You all have our blessings."

A few feeble hands applauded the fon's closing remarks. This day would indeed remain in the memories of men for many moons to come.

Chapter 13

The sun had risen high in the sky. Ngwokwong still slept. Only very few tappers were making the rounds of their palm bushes. Fomujang had been careful with his drinking the previous day and so was not as badly affected as many others. His palms were yielding abundantly. Only two showed signs of drying up already; however, if they were left untouched for some moons, they would have the chance to refill and subsequently yield plentifully again. After all, had not the people of old insisted on palms being given rests periods, during which time the gods would refill them? Fomujang wondered how his ancestors had gotten their wisdom. It occurred to him that the success of most present-day activities relied very much on the wise counselling of the people of old.

He rounded a bend and parted the grass on his path. He contemplated the *Raffia* palm before him. He stooped and moved away the palm branches to reveal a rounded calabash full to the brim with wine. He carefully lifted it and placed it on the soft grass to his right. He then took out his tapping knife and carefully scraped the bottom part of the opening on the palm stem. When he was satisfied his knife had touched all the edges of the opening, he moved it downwards and wiped off the dregs on a small palm leaf stuck into a slit on the stem. Wine from the palm flowed through the opening onto the leaf and then into the calabash.

Fomujang rose and poured the wine from the small calabash into the much larger one he had brought with him. He then replaced the small calabash under the small palm leaf. He covered the calabash and opening in the palm with palm branches, lifted the larger calabash onto his shoulder, and left.

Tita yawned – and had to grasp the wood pole by the side of his bamboo bed to hold himself steady. He sat up in his bed for a while; then he swung his legs onto the ground and rose unsteadily. He rubbed his eyes with the backs of his hands and moved to the door. He heard voices that quickly died away in the distance. He recalled how many people had been in no condition to walk back to their homes the evening before. He peered outside and squeezed his eyes to reduce the hurting rays of the morning sun. Then, suddenly, he recalled the singular event that had marked him the day before. The urgent urge to share the experience with his mother invaded him. He began to formulate in his mind the right words, when her voice broke into his thoughts.

"The day has broken, my son?"

He turned and blinked several times as he tried to readjust his eyes to the darkness in the room.

"The day has broken, Mother. You are still in bed?" He moved over and sat by her side.

"I am surprised to be up at this time. I went to bed in the early hours of this morning. I had to make sure that all our guests had places to sleep in. Did you sleep well, my son?"

"Yes, Mother." He fidgeted with his fingers before adding, "Mother I have something to tell you."

They exchanged looks, and the woman smiled with understanding. She tapped her son on the arm, "Is it about Muyang, my son?" She spoke calmly but with assurance.

Tita's eyes bulged, and he looked at her in confusion. His mouth hung open and his breathing quickened.

"It is Muyang, then?" she pressed on gently

"Yes, Mother. But who told you?"

"You did, my son. She did too."

"When was that? How? Where did I do so?" Tita frowned in his effort to recall when and where he could have mentioned Muyang's name to his mother.

"It was yesterday, my son," Tita heard his mother saying. "I was proud to hear you speak so wisely yesterday. Until then, I had been worrying and wondering whether, after all these frequent absences of yours, you would formulate the right words for your people. Did Forkon teach you what to say?"

He nodded. "But Mother, you still have not told me when I spoke to you yesterday."

"You remember when Muyang carried foofoo to the old man of Tugi?" She raised her eyebrows and looked into his eyes, her mouth curved in a crafty smile.

"Of course. Everyone saw her. She put the food down in front of him and … and …". He broke off, laughing.

"Yes, like many others, I saw the way you two exchanged looks. That spoke louder than words."

"What do you think of her?" His heartbeat went jolting again. What if she did not like her?

The woman's mind went to Zang. She had always admired Tifang's daughter and nursed the hope that one day she would bring her son to notice her and eventually take her to wife. Things had gone rather too fast and unexpectedly. She could also not go against the tradition of the land. Well, she could still try to get her as his second wife. She made up her mind then to work hard in that regard.

"I would prefer Ijang, if you want my opinion. She is smart and hard-working. Muyang is a little childish." The vein on Tita's forehead started pulsating visibly.

"I want Muyang, Mother." Determination was written all over him.

She saw no need to insist otherwise. After all, Muyang was young and from a good family. She could be groomed.

"I understand you and will support you with your choice, my son. But you must first learn fast what the elders will teach you. I can see that you will soon need your own hut."

Tita stood up and smiled down at his mother. "I am going to greet the pig."

They both laughed. He rushed out, his right palm cupping his buttocks.

Gyam hurried across the sugar-cane farm. He could hear the pig as it moved restlessly inside the bamboo fence. Everyone had been away at tawh, and so the pig had gone hungry the previous day. He came up the path and saw the animal trying to force apart two bamboo poles. Its mouth and nose were on the outside, and its body jerked violently as it tried to push its way through the fence. Gyam stamped the ground with his right foot, and the pig hastily withdrew and looked up at the newcomer. It automatically hurried away to position itself under the flat stone towards which Gyam was moving. Quickly, the man pulled away his loincloth and squatted on the stone. The veins on his neck swelled as he pushed the waste from his bowels out and down into the waiting mouth of the pig below. Two more lumps left his body, and he sighed with relief. His body relaxed, and his mind drifted onto the events of the previous day. He wondered whether he had ever witnessed a greater occasion in Ngwokwong or in any of the neighbouring villages in his entire life.

His thoughts shifted to his friend, Mukom. He had left him still snoring on the mat a while ago. Twice he had tried to wake him, but each time Mukom tried to raise his body, he had fallen back, groaning. Well, Gyam smiled to himself, his friend would remember Ngwokwong for a long time to come. His knees began to ache. He satisfied himself that he had freed himself of the unwanted load and that nothing more would come out of his body. He stretched out his hand, broke off some soft grass beside him, and cleaned himself up. He picked up his loincloth and tied it around his middle as he peered at the pig. It sniffed and groaned, clearly expecting more.

"Are you sorry to have given that pig very little food?"

Gyam saw Mukom unsteadily walking towards him.

"From the way you are walking, I think you are carrying enough load to keep it hunger-free for two full moons." Gyam stepped away to make way for the newcomer. "I better rush off now, if I still want my nose to be able to distinguish between the Ngwokwong wine and the Tugi water that you call *Raffia* wine."

Mukom squatted, and a black evil-smelling lump came out almost immediately. He was still so unsteady that he had to support himself on all ten fingers.

Gyam covered his nose as he walked away. "Beware you don't throw yourself onto the mud below."

Tifang walked unsteadily to the door. Gyam stood at the threshold and watched, amused.

"At last the day has broken? Did you sleep well?"

Tifang was still rubbing his eyes as he asked, "Is the sun up yet? Bees seem to have invaded my head. I wonder how I am going to trek back to Zang."

Gyam twitched his mouth as he observed the other squeezing the loincloth between his thighs. "Have bees gone in there, too? Oh! I believe you want to pass out the leftover of yesterday's wine."

The urge in Tifang's kidneys increased, and he pushed past Gyam and hurried to the back of the hut.

"Be careful not to destroy the cocoyam leaves," Gyam said as he crossed the threshold. He moved close to the fireside and pulled a stool towards him. Tengu adjusted the wood under her pot.

"What are you already cooking, Muyang's mother?"

"Have you visited your palm bush? I am just heating up the leftover yam porridge from yesterday. You know that our guests will soon want to leave."

"Ha ha. I am still waiting for that man who will argue against the strength of Ngwokwong wine."

Gyam spread his hands over the pot and sighed as his body warmed up. At that moment, Fomujang walked in and lowered the calabash from his shoulder. Tengu pushed a stool over to him.

"Please bring the kettle."

Tengu rose to get it.

"I saw Tifang outside. Has Mukom left?" Fomujang asked as he took the kettle from Tengu.

"Would that not go against what our fathers used to say?" Mukom spoke as he stepped in, followed by Tifang. Gyam looked up at his friend.

"You feel much better now, I suppose. I hope you did not punish the pig with that huge load you carried? So you, even, know our fathers' sayings?"

"Chaah, Gyam," Tifang said with a giggle, tapping Gyam on the back, "you are behaving like a monkey that senses the approach of a hunter. How would you think that a great man like Mukom could ignore the wisdom of our forefathers?"

"That is what he told me." Gyam said, rubbing his stomach distractedly.

Mukom started to protest, when Tengu intervened. "I know men do not speak with wisdom when their stomachs are empty. Food will soon be ready. Do not pour wine into empty stomachs."

"Wise words, aboh. I hope my friend here will hear and learn." Mukom rubbed his chin and beamed. He tapped Gyam lightly on the back and added, "Maybe I should teach you the other saying, for I can see you have difficulty to admit you do not know."

"If you say it correctly, I can promise you two cups of our wine before you set off on your return journey to that Tugi land where all palms have dried up."

Fomujang had filled the kettle with wine. Gyam picked it up and placed it on the logs.

Tengu pushed a bowl of vegetables and a basket with hot yams towards the men.

"You should stop talking and enjoy your meal."

Mukom moved his stool closer. "Thank you, great woman! There is no need wasting energy to teach Gyam, for he does not understand a thing, particularly when his stomach is empty."

Fomujang removed the kettle from the fire and poured some wine into his horn. There was silence as he stepped to the door.

"Our forefathers and protectors of these lands, partake of your children's meal." He poured half the contents of his horn onto the ground and moved back to his seat. Tengu filled the horns of the men, and they ate with visible appetite.

"I am feeling better now," Mukom declared, his mouth full with food.

"You can't feel otherwise when you are eating food prepared by Muyang's mother and drinking Ngwokwong wine. I am sure Tifang is of the same opinion?"

Gyam nodded in the direction of Tifang. The latter noisily chewed a mouthful of vegetable. "I should really be going now. Thank you for the wonderful meal, Tengu."

Fomujang raised his eyes from the bowl and stared significantly at him. Tifang understood that His friend meant him to hold on a little longer. Mukom wiped his hands on his legs and emptied his horn.

"I should be going too. That lazy son of mine would not even think of repairing the opening on my pig's fence."

"Seeing the rate at which pigs are speared to death these days, you really should hurry. But don't fail to invite me to eat some of it if it gets killed," Gyam said, his mouth full.

"My brother has spoken wisely. I hope, though, that you do not really mean to eat up my pig."

Mukom then turned to Tengu and expressed his gratitude as he stood up to leave. "May the gods pour more blessings on you and your family. Thank you for refilling my stomach, Tengu. May our ancestors continue to replenish our *Raffia* palms."

"You mean the Ngwokwong palms, don't you?" Gyam cut in.

"Instead of tickling me, get up and escort me." He caught Gyam's hand.

"Are you sure you don't want to fill your horn again?" Gyam filled his friends' horn.

"This is to clear your sight as you walk home," Gyam stated, like a physician to a patient. He filled his own horn, and together the two men left. Their voices soon faded away in the distance.

Tifang shook his head slowly. "With those two by one's side, no serious work can be done. You don't even have the chance to say a thing."

"They have their own usefulness, though." Fomujang noted.

"Did your son tell you where he was going to pass the night?" Tengu asked her husband. "I haven't seen him since last evening."

"He did not have to. I believe he passed the night at Sango's."

"That son of yours is one to be proud of. Yesterday he performed so well that I began to wonder if he had not eaten the heart of a gorilla." Tifang nodded with admiration.

Tengu jumped from her stool. "Are you saying that it was my son that was dressed up in that frightful mask?"

"So, you could not recognise your son's shape and movements? I would recognise him amongst a hundred masks," Fomujang remarked with a touch of pride.

"When you make decisions in the council, do you share them with us?"

"We do not have to tell our women everything. We tell them what they need to know. Aha! You remind me of the meeting we have this afternoon in tawh."

"If I had a son, I would be the happiest man," Tifang said sadly.

"You forget that Nande is the pride of your compound? I can even say the pride of all Zang," Fomujang spoke, but he wondered how it really felt to have no male heir.

"Chaah!" Tifang exclaimed and stood up. "Isn't today the day after ko'o?"

"What about it?" Gyam spoke from the door. "Ooh! you mean the day we are to meet our daughter? I was—"

He stopped and smiled uncomfortably at Tengu. She was staring up at him, her mouth quietly widening.

Tensed silence fell into the room. "What are you talking about? Tengu hissed.

The men exchanged looks but none opted to respond.

"For the past days, I have felt that something was going on and no one would tell me what about," Tengu went on indignantly.

"You are right," Fomujang confirmed. Then, choosing his words carefully, he related to her the events of the past days.

When he stopped, Tengu held her head in her palms. "And to think that my son could not confide in me." She clapped her hands in disappointment.

"He obviously wanted to, Muyang's mother. But we thought that with the recent events we were all involved in, you might have too many things on your mind," Gyam pleaded in earnest.

There was some silence, and then someone coughed from the door. Akatcho moved in and sat on the bamboo bed. "Mother, I had wanted to tell you the other day when I complained of headache. It wasn't headache at all." Akatcho paused and looked at his father.

"We can understand that you had headache." Gyam was not very sure what to say.

"I would have told you, Mother. But Father had told me to hold on till after the ceremony yesterday."

Tengu visibly relaxed. "So, you were really the one wearing that terrible mask?"

The young man smiled and nodded. He looked at his father again, hoping he would say something to reassure his mother. Fomujang shifted on his stool and picked up the kettle from the floor. It felt very light. He held it in front of his son. The latter showed his horn, and the contents of the kettle were emptied into it. Dregs half filled the horn. Akatcho looked with disgust into his horn.

"Drink that, my child. That will prove very useful sooner than later," Gyam encouraged the young man.

Still Fomujang said nothing. Tengu was burning with the desire to know more.

"Who is she, my son?"

For answer, Akatcho nodded in the direction of Tifang. The woman understood. She closed her eyes as Nande's profile came into her mind. Akatcho misunderstood his mother's attitude and threw an imploring look at his father. He needed to say something to calm her. The older man smiled with assurance at his son.

Tengu opened her eyes and faced the gaze of the four men in the room. She shifted her eyes onto her husband and slowly nodded with approval. "I like my daughter Nande," she said calmly.

All four men heaved a sigh of relief.

Chapter 14

The ten elders sat in the tawh hall. They hardly talked as they sipped from their horns. From the anxious looks they threw at the door, it was plain that they were expecting someone. Tita's mother walked into the hall. She stooped, her hands joined in front of her, as she crossed the room and took up her seat by her son's side. She rubbed her palms together and clapped, the men joining in, in the traditional salute.

Forkon cleared his throat and looked outside. "It will soon be time for some of us to tend to our palms. I hope we will be brief."

Andang stood up and began filling the horns in the room. Forkon noticed that Tita's mother did not have her little calabash. He beckoned her, and she moved over in the same stooping manner. When she took the cup offered to her, she dropped onto her knees before drinking down its content. She emptied another horn full before moving back to her stool.

"The first thing we shall discuss is what we expect our son to tell us," Forkon began.

The pairs of eyes turned and settled on Tita. The boy tightened his grip on the horn to keep his hands steady.

"You have caught the animal, haven't you?" Azoh asked.

Tita nodded.

"Which is it?"

The boy raised his eyes and let them wander round the room. They settled on Fomujang and stayed there for a while before dropping. The men followed the gesture. Things were taking shape.

"Tell us her name," Abanda urged gently.

"Muyang."

There was a general movement as the men adjusted themselves on their stools and exchanged looks. To hide his confusion, Fomujang raised his horn to his mouth.

"Your son's eyes are good. What do you say, Tita's mother?"

Forkon had watched the woman but had seen no signs of what was going on in her mind. Her voice was steady when she spoke. "Does a tree stop the wind from its course? Besides, I like my daughter, Muyang."

"Then, to simplify things," Forkon went on, "we shall proceed as befits our tradition. However, no tree bears fruit until it has matured. Shall we proceed, Fomujang?"

Fomujang swallowed the wine he held meditatively in his mouth and wiped his mouth with the back of his left hand. He remembered the belief of their ancestors that the gods pointed out to a fon who his wife should be. Tita was full of uncertainty. Nevertheless, who was he to go against the choice of the gods?

"It is indeed an honour for me that my daughter has caught the heart of Tita. I, however, would like to advise our son to be sure of his feelings for my daughter, because a man's first wife represents the stability of his home. And in this special circumstance, I mean the stability and happiness of Ngwokwong."

The men in the room nodded with approval as Fomujang signalled to Forkon that his speech had ended. All eyes settled on Tita once more.

"I love Muyang very much," he answered the silent question on the men's faces.

"We must thank our gods that no obstacle stands in the way thus far. Before we carry on to other discussions, we would like our son to go and discuss this matter with his mother."

The others mumbled their approval of Abanda's words.

"That I have done, my fathers. But there is something I am worried about." Tita rubbed his palms, as if uncertain how to voice his worry.

"Confide in your fathers, my son," his mother urged.

"When shall I go for my cows?" he asked abruptly.

The men shifted uneasily on their stools. Was he seeking a way to leave his home again? Forkon turned to Abanda, and they exchanged views in low tones. Then Abanda raised his voice so all could hear.

"We understand your problem, my son. Some of your brothers will follow you the day after tomorrow to help bring your cows home."

"I thank you, my fathers." Tita smiled. He was relieved and happy. He stood up and moved out with his mother.

As soon as they were some distance from the hall, Tita turned to his mother. "I am going to the palm bush, Mother."

"Where is your knife and calabash?" She looked a little surprised at him.

"Oh, I will first go for a walk. I will tap later."

Before the woman could say more, he had hurried away. She sensed the excitement in him and that he was trying to conceal something.

Tita walked towards the stream. He was lost in thought. The conversation in the hall some minutes earlier filled his mind again. He was excited at the idea of Muyang becoming his wife. When would he meet her? If only he could see her now. He walked past a compound. He did not know whose it was. He walked on, his mind so jammed that he did not hear footsteps behind him. Someone coughed, and he quivered with fright, coming back to the present. He turned round and faced Muyang. His heart leaped within him.

For a moment they stared at each other in surprise.

"Where are you coming from?" he quickly recovered enough to ask.

"From that compound. That is where my friend lives." Muyang's voice was hardly audible.

"And who is that friend of yours?"

"Ijang."

Tita had unconsciously edged closer. She began to fidget with a blade of grass.

142

"Muyang." He heard his own voice. The girl looked up at him shyly.

"I … I want to … tell you something."

He was annoyed with himself for not getting his words smoothly. His heart started racing and his breathing quickened.

"What is it?" Muyang stammered.

Tita swallowed the saliva that seemed to stop the words coming out of his mouth. His right fingers started stroking the same blade of grass Muyang was fidgeting with.

"You will be my wife?"

His voice was husky. Muyang shivered, and her eyes widened.

"Your wife? I do not know. My father will—".

"Do you like me?" he asked, his voice trembling.

She nodded but started twisting her fingers, looking embarrassed and confused.

"But I fear, should my father know."

"He knows." Tita began to recover and gain control of himself.

She trembled visibly. Her eyes asked the question which her mouth could not formulate.

"All the elders know. I am just from the council. They asked me whom I have chosen as my first wife. You are the only one who filled my thoughts. I told them so."

"My father was there?"

"Yes. He did not oppose the idea. The elders said I have good eyes."

She smiled and started breathing normally again. "I should be going now," she said looking up at him.

Without warning, he caught her in his arms and pressed her against his body. In his excitement, he did not realise she might feel pain. His muscles swelled as he pressed her harder. She groaned with pain.

"Oh! They will see us. Let me go now."

Reluctantly he dropped his hands to his sides. "I will see you tomorrow?"

Muyang was already moving away. She stopped, nodded to him, and then hurried off. Tita was almost shouting with joy. It was as if a weight had been lifted from his shoulders. Was there any reason to continue in the direction of the stream? He looked up at the sky and almost closed his eyes, as the sun's heat was reaching its maximum intensity. If only the wishes of men could always be realised so smoothly and quickly. He turned his steps homewards. He needed to share this with his mother. He had forgotten about his palm bush.

Fomujang sat opposite his wife. They were in earnest discussion when Muyang arrived.

"At last you are back, my child. You did not tell me you would stay this long." Tengu affectionately pulled her daughter to her side. She immediately sensed the suppressed excitement in the girl. It could not be caused by the presence of her father, she thought.

"What have you been doing at your friend's home?" Fomujang asked calmly.

"Ijang's mother taught us how to weave baskets."

"Your father wants to talk to you." Muyang noted the anxiety on her mother's face. She knew at once what her father was about to discuss.

"Many people told me yesterday that you have taken after your mother with the art of cooking." Fomujang tried to be tactful. He quickly realised that he did not have Gyam's talent of introducing such topics indirectly. He decided to act in his normal fashion.

"Tita wants you for his wife."

Father and mother looked at their daughter anxiously. There was neither surprise nor fear on her face. "I met him near the stream as I came home." She began to pull her fingers nervously.

"Did he talk with you?" Tengu asked. The girl nodded.

"What did you talk about? Did you two plan to meet?"

Fomujang's brows began to gather.

"No," Muyang said quickly, "I met him by chance as I came home from Ijang's."

"What did you talk about?" Fomujang repeated his question.

"He told me that he likes me. And that you have discussed it in the council."

The frown was still on Fomujang's face.

"It was not for him to tell you about this. He should have allowed me to talk with you first. However, what do you think of him?"

"I … I like him too," she murmured.

There was silence as each person wrestled with varying thoughts.

The men moved on in silence, one behind the other. The sun was fast getting overhead. Its heat had increased enormously. The grazing cows raised their heads to look at the passers-by. Akatcho led the way. He walked with quick, bouncy steps. The jug of wine he carried on his shoulder did not seem to weigh on him. The sweat running down his face was caused more by the heat of the sun. Sango followed him closely. They exchanged the jug at regular intervals. Behind him came Fomujang. Farther behind was Gyam, who had at some point branched off the path to relieve himself. He tried to catch up with the others, but they moved too quickly for his liking. He decided to engage them in a conversation. That should slow the pace a little, he convinced himself.

"Hey! Have you forgotten I am travelling with you?"

Fomujang waited for him, his brows gathered and his eyes focussed on the ground. As Gyam came nearer, he realised that his friend was deep in thought.

"You are not debating with yourself whether to go back or to move on, I hope?"

"No, not that. I have this uneasy feeling of an alluring ill omen. Don't you think it would have been wise to take one witness on this expedition?"

Gyam looked at the sky and then behind him.

"You are not thinking of going back all the way, and under this scorching heat, to look for a witness, I hope?

"How can I go all the way back? I am not thinking of that. Rather, I am thinking that Awah should be our man. What do you say?"

"You are right. I think a witness from Zang will show wisdom on our part. Did not our fathers say that the dog that watches its bone every day is better placed to defend it than the one that only hears of it?"

Fomujang smiled with satisfaction. He turned, and they moved on. "I will branch off somewhere ahead and take the path towards Awah's compound. I think you shall need to go on with the boys."

"Let's hope the wine Awah drank in Ngwokwong is still weighing him down. Else you would not meet him at home at this time of the day," Gyam said with a chuckle.

The young men had disappeared in the distance. They made their way quickly around the huts, wondering whether anyone would be at home at that time of day. When they arrived at Tifang's compound, they noticed the smoke from the thatched-roofed hut. They sighed with relief. Someone was certainly at home.

"Who is in?" Akatcho called out.

"Who is asking questions as though he were a stranger?" a female voice responded from the hut. Akatcho recognised the voice at once. He winked at his friend.

"Will you not come out to receive your strangers?"

The girl appeared at the threshold. "*Yeeeeh!* Is it you?" She covered her mouth with her right hand, surprised.

"You were not expecting us?" Sango asked, smiling at her.

"I was expecting people. Father told me this morning not to go out because he was expecting visitors. It did not cross my mind that you would be the ones."

"Where is Mother?" Akatcho asked.

"She is behind the compound. Father did not want her to go to her farm today."

"What are you cooking?" Sango enquired.

"I am boiling cocoyam to pound foofoo." She stared past the boys.

"Aha, wonderful! My favourite food. You knew I was coming along, my daughter?" Gyam dragged himself up past the boys to Nande's side.

"I am almost completely dehydrated. Is your father at home, my child?"

"Yes. He is mending the pig's fence. He asked me to call for him when you arrive."

"Run and tell him that I am roasting alive."

She smiled at the boys and disappeared round the hut. Gyam tapped Akatcho on the shoulder and winked in the direction the girl had gone. Akatcho looked at his friend. The latter urged him on with a light push. Akatcho hurried after her.

"You children of today do not even know the basics of courtship. In my days, h'm, before the girls realised what was happening, they were already in our bags. The wine and talking came later. Today it is the reverse. Well, let us go and sit down, my son.

They moved into the hut.

Chapter 15

"Hey! Will you not wait for me?"

Nande stopped and turned around. Akatcho was coming up quickly towards her. They were quite a distance from her father's compound. As she stood there watching his approach, her heart began to pound in her ribs. Akatcho walked up to her, and they stood looking at each other. His lips parted but no sound came out. He could hear his own heartbeat. Unable to formulate the right words, Akatcho began to lose temper with himself. At that moment, his father's words came into his mind: "You are a man now. You must not show fear or weakness before a woman." His eyes bulged a little under the pressure from within.

"Why do you look at me like that?" He heard her voice from a distance.

"I like you." His voice was a little hoarse. He knew no other way at that moment of voicing his feelings.

"Is that why you came to Zang?"

"Yes. You don't like our coming?"

"I like your coming."

He wanted her to say more. Instead she fidgeted with her fingers. "Do you like me?" he asked eagerly.

She looked up at him and nodded. Their eyes locked. He stepped closer, and his hands went round her in a timid embrace. He felt her warm breath against his hairless chest.

"I want you to be my wife. Would you be happy if we spent the rest of our lives together?"

Her voice was low and calm but transmitted the determination that had formed within her. "I will be nobody else's wife."

He tightened his embrace.

Sango poured the wine from the jug into the clay pot which Tifang had placed at the centre of the room. Five men and a woman sat around the pot. After Sango had resumed his position, silence followed. After a while, Fomujang cleared his throat, and attention shifted to him.

"My brother Tifang, this is not the first time we are all sitting together. Yesterday we were all drinking wine from the same pot in Ngwokwong. Here we are today, still looking forward to sharing, even though the wine in the pots represents different matters. My brothers, each day that brings men together also gives them the things to talk about."

He searched the faces of the others before settling on Tifang. "The plantain sucker you planted some years back has grown and is catching the eye of all who come around your compound. I have come to ask for a sucker from that grown plantain stem to plant in my own compound. Did not our fathers say that a man should share with his friends that which makes the pride of his compound?" Fomujang folded his arms across his chest and sought approval from the others with raised eyebrows.

Tifang sat up on his stool and adjusted the loincloth between his thighs. He watched on as the others nodded in approval of Fomujang's words. His mind began to search for the right response. When he made up his mind, he raised his head.

"I have heard my brother Fomujang's words. I know that the events of yesterday in Ngwokwong have drained some energy from us, and our bodies need rest. However, if you have decided to ignore your tiredness and travel all this way to my compound, I can appreciate the importance you attach to your mission."

Tifang stopped and sipped from his horn. "Our fathers used to say that when a man finishes building his house and does not move in, the rat mole soon will make it its home and may even start its family."

He turned to his wife. "Do you have anything to add, Engoneb?"

Tifang's wife clapped her hands and tilted her head sideways as she spoke, "When a young bird has developed its wings, can a mother oblige it to stay at home?"

"Well spoken, Nande's mother," Gyam intervened excitedly. "Not only has the bird you allude to developed wings, but they are the brightest ones in all of Zang land."

Akatcho half followed the conversation. On the one hand, he was not quite conversant with the use of proverbs, and on the other hand, part of his mind had gone out in search of Nande. When his father spoke, he did not realise he was talking to him. Sango nudged his friend to bring him to the present.

"Will you fill your father's horn?" Fomujang repeated, looking at his son and pointing in Tifang's direction. Akatcho moved over, picked up the calabash, and filled Tifang's horn. The latter stood up and walked to the door. He poured half the contents of the horn over the threshold.

"Our forefathers," he murmured, "may you witness and bless this day."

Fomujang took out a large piece of kola nut and gave it to his son to take to Tifang. The latter rubbed it between his palms and then squeezed, his mouth twisting with the effort. The nut split into five pieces. He held them in his outstretched right palm. Fomujang, Awah, Gyam, and Engoneb picked a piece each. Tifang threw the last one into his mouth and held his horn in front of him. Akatcho hurried over and filled it with the wine he had brought. He filled it two more times, and then Tifang sighed and smiled.

"Ngwokwong wine, I do not know what it is you put into your wine to make it so good. Go and serve your fathers, my son."

"We are overlooking one important step. Where is my daughter?" Fomujang remarked as Akatcho filled his horn.

"The most important step has been taken, hasn't it?" Tifang wondered.

"We must not neglect the least of the rules of our ancestors," Fomujang said firmly.

Tifang shrugged and then nodded to his wife. She left and almost immediately reappeared, with Nande following her.

"It looks as if she has been standing behind the door. She must be very eager to be near you. My congratulations again for your brilliant choice," Sango whispered to Akatcho.

"Come and drink from your father's cup, my child."

Tifang held his horn in front of him. Nande took the horn in both palms and sipped from it.

"Would you take the horn to any person you like in this room?" Tifang urged her.

The girl moved over to Fomujang and handed him the cup. Gyam smiled broadly and winked at Engoneb. The older woman had done her homework properly. It would have been embarrassing had she handed the horn to Akatcho.

Fomujang emptied the contents, and his face lit up with one of his rare smiles.

"I am happy, my daughter. Tell your father that I would only really be happy if he allows you to fill my cup every day."

The girl conveyed the message. Then her mother signalled her to follow her. The two women left the room. Gyam turned to the two young men and made faces at them.

"Call me a liar if I say that you don't have things to say to the pride of Zang. She has them full in her basket, and you, I believe, have them full in your bags."

"You may go outside, young men, if you wish and have stories to share." Awah spoke for the first time.

"Can a man ever lack stories to tell a woman?" Gyam wondered with apparent sincerity. The men burst out laughing.

Akatcho caught Sango's hand, and they walked out of the room.

The news of Muyang's engagement to Tita had spread like wildfire in the *harmattan*. Since his return from Zang seven days earlier, Fomujang had been actively involved in the arrangements for the impending marriage that would unite his daughter to the fon-to-be. His thoughts were divided. On the one hand, he was proud that his daughter was going to be the first wife to Tita, with all that it implied. On the other hand, he was worried about the young man's character. If he proved to be a nuisance, then he would be sending his daughter into boiling oil. He had discussed his fear with Forkon.

The latter had simply remarked, "No worthy father allows his son to go astray. We must mould him into a man fit to look after his people."

The day chosen for Muyang's hand to be officially asked for in marriage was fast approaching. She had insisted that her brother's wife-to-be should live with her for some time. Tifang did not refuse when Fomujang posed the suggestion. He did warn, however, that the two young people be watched closely, for as he put it, "No fruit is good when plucked unripe from the tree."

Akatcho had no single moment alone with Nande. She was always either with Muyang or her mother or both. He saw her every day, however, and that kept his anxiety under control. The two girls loved and respected each other. They seemed to differ, though, in their perceptions of the physical prowess of their respective husbands-to-be. Their conversation always revolved around the two young men.

"Soon you will be wearing white beads around your head," Nande said teasingly.

"You like my brother, eh?" Muyang asked.

"Akatcho is very powerful. He lifts me up like a leaf. Is Tita equally strong?"

"I am convinced he is more powerful than my brother. You just need to see his chest to know that."

"I think you are exaggerating his strength. No boy of Akatcho's age can throw him to the ground. He told me so himself." Nande's confidence somehow irritated Muyang.

"I wish they could wrestle so that you might see for yourself. I would like to visit his mother this afternoon. You will come with me? Perhaps, if you are lucky, you will see him, too."

By the time the two girls walked into tawh, most of the women had returned from their farms. Tita's mother was adjusting the pot over the fire when the two girls crossed the threshold.

"Welcome, my daughter. Who is that with you?" She wiped the tears from her eyes. "This smoke will soon blind me."

Muyang introduced her friend. "This is Nande, Tifang's daughter."

"Chaah! The smoke has so affected my eyes that I could not recognise my own daughter. Aboh, come and sit down by my side."

The woman sent her hand around the girl in a warm motherly embrace. "You would not believe me, but I have been thinking about you and your mother. How is my namesake?"

"She is well. So you have the same name as my mother?" Nande looked pleasantly surprised.

"My daughter, not too many people know me by my name." The woman added, throwing a knowing smile at Muyang, "In a couple of years from now, my daughter, Muyang, might even have forgotten her own name."

Tita's mother was hardly ever called by her name. It was customary to refer to the fon's wife as the mother of this or that of her children. The link was usually associated with the first child.

"Where is Tita, Mother?" Muyang asked, rubbing her eyes with the backs of her hands. She was still standing.

"Why not sit down, my child? You see the smoke is going upwards."

"What animal is that over the fire, Mother?" Nande asked, feeling quite at home in the older woman's embrace.

"That is a rat mole that Tita caught in his trap this morning."

"Where has he gone to, Mother?" Muyang repeated her question.

"I am here." Tita spoke from the door. He moved in, looked searchingly at Nande, and then raised his brows at Muyang.

"This is Nande. The one I talked to you the other day about."

"So you are the one that captured Akatcho's heart?" Tita spoke as Muyang pushed a stool towards him.

Tita's mother caught her breath sharply. Her hand fell limply from Nande's shoulder.

"What is it, Mother?" Tita jumped from his seat, alarmed. Muyang was also up in an instant, and her eyes widened in fear. Nande's right hand stretched towards the older woman, preparing to support her physically if it became necessary.

"Something got into my eye," the woman lied, covering her right eye with her left palm. She rose unsteadily to her feet. "I will be all right. Let me go and get this dirt out of my eye. You girls take care of the pot on the fire."

Tita made to follow her, but she laid a restraining hand on him. "I will be all right. Keep company to my young daughters."

She made her way to the back of the hut, and her brows gathered in thought, following what she had just learnt. Did that explain Fomujang's frequent visits to Zang? She had not paid much attention to them. She knew of Fomujang's friendship with Awah. She had also believed that the visits were more in connection with the recent happenings in Ngwokwong. She cursed herself for not having acted earlier. What if Fomujang had already carried the customary wine to Tifang? Here she was, all the time thinking of Nande as the ideal wife for her son. She would have preferred Nande as her son's first wife, had tradition not been in her way. However, she had promised herself that she would encourage her son to marry her as his second wife. She was almost slipping into tears when an idea struck her. She turned and hurried back into the hut.

"Aboh, you told me the other day that your father went to Zang. Was he alone?"

The young people exchanged looks. Then Muyang realised the question was directed at her. "He went with Gyam, Akatcho, and Sango. Did you get the dirt out of your eye, Mother?"

Muyang could sense some tension in the woman's voice.

"I am all right, my child. You are certain no one else went along with them?" the woman enquired again, her lips trembling slightly.

"I am sure. Mother, is there something wrong?"

Muyang's face clearly showed the worry building up inside her.

Tita's mother realised it was time to diffuse the tension that was gradually rising. "No, my child, I just remembered that I sent Tita's younger brother, Mbah, to someone's home, and he did not meet him on that same day your father went to Zang. I thought they might have gone together."

Nande was not comfortable with the conversation. She sat with respectful silence, however. Tita hung his *Raffia* bag on the bamboo wall. He was sure something was worrying his mother. He promised himself to pull it from her as soon as the others had left.

"Where are you coming from?" Muyang asked him as the older woman turned her attention to the pot on the fire.

"I went to tend to my *Raffia* palms. So, this is Nande! Is she staying with you?"

"Yes. She has been …". Her voice trailed off as she saw the cut on Tita's leg. "Heh! What happened to your leg?" Muyang's face clouded with concern.

Nande turned on her stool and peered at the cut. "What have you applied to it?"

"Mother squeezed some green liquid into it yesterday. I never felt pain like it before, when that liquid dropped onto the gash."

Tita's mother went on with her cooking, apparently oblivious to what was going on around her. Her mind certainly was elsewhere.

"Did you cut yourself with a knife?" Muyang massaged gently the area round the cut.

"No. Let me tell you the story. Yesterday, as we led my cows homewards, at one point one of them went berserk and charged unexpectedly at me. I dived sideways to avoid its horns, but unfortunately, my leg hit the sharp edge of a stone. The cow kept advancing, and I was unable to rise."

The girls drew in their breaths sharply. That brought the older woman back to the present.

She stood up. "Food is ready. Go ahead and serve yourselves. I want to go over to Forkon." She wore a smile as she turned towards Tita and Muyang.

"You know we have to start making the necessary arrangements for you two, don't you? I will not be long." She apparently was not expecting any answer, as she stepped outside.

"How did you then escape its horns?" Nande asked eagerly. Muyang covered her mouth with her right palm as if trying to stifle a scream.

"Your brother is a brave man," Tita said, looking at Muyang. "When he saw me lying helplessly, he ran and leapt onto the cow's back and held fast to its horns. The animal became furious and ran madly around, trying to shake off its assailant. When the other boys with us had helped me safely over a fence close by, I saw Akatcho jump to the ground. Before the cow could turn round to attack him, he had climbed into a tree like a monkey. The cow stood under the tree looking up at him. The next moment, Akatcho took a thick coil of rope from his bag and made a loop, which he threw around the cow's neck. When he had tied the rope round the tree, he climbed down and joined me. I was thereafter supported back home."

Nande's face radiated with pride.

"So, Akatcho did not even fear that the cow would harm him?"

"I admire your brother's courage and daring." He rubbed Muyang's hand to lift her spirits. "You are lucky to have him as your future husband." He smiled at Nande.

Muyang twisted her mouth in contempt as she recalled her previous conversation with Nande. "You are not saying that my brother is stronger than you? It was just that you cut your leg – else you would have overcome the cow, wouldn't you?"

"If I had not cut my leg, I suppose I would have run out of reach of the animal. I am not comparing strength with your brother, though. He saved me from a difficult situation."

"Could you throw Akatcho to the ground in a wrestling bout?" Muyang pressed on.

Tita's face clouded perceptibly. "I do not wish an occasion to arise for that. I do not fear him. I respect him."

Nande sensed the atmosphere tightening. She said quickly, "It is getting dark outside. Shall we go now, Muyang?"

"Will you still be around in the next two days?" Tita asked, looking at Nande, as the two girls rose to go.

"What is going to happen in the next two days?" Nande asked with a crafty smile and pulled Muyang away. Tita reluctantly let go the girl's hand. They three broke out laughing.

"Are you serious about leaving? I am so hungry. What about you?"

"Oh! Let me get you something to eat." Muyang pulled her friend back and urged her to sit while she looked for the bowl to dish out food for him. They all sat down and enjoyed their meal before the two girls left.

Chapter 16

The sun had not risen yet. The birds sang noisily, marking the early hours of the morning. It was quite cold, but Tita's mother hurried on. She had covered a great distance, and her loincloth was covered with dew. She had left her hut unseen after the second crow of the cock. She had to act fast, before it became too late – if it was not already. As the first rays of the sun burst over the horizon, she walked into Tifang's compound. When the latter saw the woman standing at his doorway, his mouth widened in surprise. He had been filing his machete, preparing to leave for his farm.

"Tita's mother? Is it really you?" he stammered.

"It is me, all right. If I have come to you without warning, you can imagine the worm that is eating me up." She entered the hut and then seemed to recall something. "Chaah! I have just started talking without first greeting you."

Tifang pushed a stool towards his guest. "Forget about the greeting. What has happened?" His voice trembled with the fear that was quickly building up within him.

"Nothing!" She sat down. "Where is my namesake?"

"She has just left for her farm. I was getting ready to join her on the farm." Tifang looked at the floor, his mind in turmoil. If anything had happened to his daughter, he was telling himself, she would not be the one to come to inform him. However, everything is possible, he thought with dismay.

"My daughter is with Fomujang. Did she come to visit you?"

"I am here because of your daughter." She spoke calmly but firmly.

"What has happened to her?" Tifang began to rise from his chair, sick with worry.

"You needn't worry. My daughter is well and strong." She shifted her stool closer to the man. "I hope there is *no smoke in the house*?"

"No, I am the only one at home. Nande's sisters have gone to pick palm kernels."

"Tell me. Has Fomujang visited you with the customary jug of wine?"

There was unmistakable anxiety in her voice. Tifang's brows gathered. He tried to understand what the woman was driving at. How could it interest her that he had received the customary jug?

"Has he?" she reiterated her question.

He nodded slowly.

"Oh, Tifang!" She beat her thighs with her palms dejectedly. She broke into sobs.

"I do not understand." Tifang's heart began to beat unsteadily.

"I have always considered Nande as my daughter-in-law. You know that I am a daughter of Zang. I know that the best women come from here. I have secretly nursed the wish to have Tita take his wife from here. Nande caught my interest many moons back. And now to know that Fomujang has preceded me is unbearable."

"Why did you not come earlier?" Tifang still could not make sense of what she was telling him.

"How was I to know when my son would finally settle in his home?" She spread her hands helplessly. There was silence for a few moments.

"I fear it is too late."

"Who came along with Fomujang?" she enquired, her lips trembling. "I mean, who was his witness?

"Nobody came from Ngwokwong other than Gyam, Sango and Akatcho. But Awah was here as witness."

"I want you to help an old widow. Will you help me?" she entreated.

"How can I undo what has been done?"

"You would not want your daughter to be the most respected woman in Ngwokwong?"

"If I wanted it, how could I change the situation? After all, aren't we hearing of the impending marriage of your son to Fomujang's daughter?"

"My son was forced to take her to wife," she lied. "You know how influential Forkon is. He insisted that my son's first wife come from Ngwokwong. But it is your daughter my son wants – and needs. Do you understand?"

"Well, I think Forkon is just respecting the tradition. But when did your son begin telling you of his feelings for Nande?"

"Just when he returned home," she said immediately. "Since the elders forced Muyang unto him, he has not slept well. He keeps telling me it is Nande he wants. What could a poor widow do? You are the only one to help me."

Tifang was looking dreamingly at the bamboo ceiling. He did not see the corn and soot that hung from it. If only she had come earlier, he kept telling himself. The idea of his daughter becoming a fon's wife and one of the foremost of the women appealed to him very strongly. Nande was his first and only grown-up daughter. It had taken seven years for her to get a little sister and four more to get a second one. Who knew whether he would be alive to see his two little girls get married to suitable husbands. At least he was alive now, and his daughter must get the best husband. He thought of the preferential treatment that would be given him whenever he visited her. He saw himself in tawh hall in Ngwokwong, surrounded by the elders, each with a calabash of wine to welcome him. He smiled as his mind wandered, unconscious of the watching eyes of the woman by his side.

A small hand touched his knee. He jumped slightly, coming back to the present.

"How shall we rearrange things?" he asked, his voice coming from a distance. Evidently, his selfish thoughts had overcome his will power.

The woman spoke fast. Her voice was clearer and stronger. "Let's think of it this way," she began, examining her fingers. "My late husband carried the jug of wine to you, engaging Nande to his son. The boy left the village suddenly. His father left us. You did not think that the boy would turn up again, still asking for Nande's hand." She stopped and looked up enquiringly.

"What a woman you are! Everything seems to fall in place. But when shall I tell the story?" Tifang was looking with admiration at the woman.

She thought for a while. "In two days' time," she said, "Muyang will be sworn in as my son's first wife. If you turn up then, I think things would not be difficult."

Tifang silently stood up and moved into his inner room. He came back with a small calabash of palm wine, which he held in front of her. She clapped her hands and showed him her palms.

"Oh!" he said, smiling. "I forgot that an ant bit you, and you forgot your little basket as you escaped."

She laughed and accepted the horn he gave her. "You know I did not tell anybody that I was coming here."

"I hope the road will not be too long now." Tifang filled the horn.

"How can it, when you have put real energy into my feet and heart? I will be waiting for you, eh?"

He nodded. She emptied two horns in succession and then stood up. The sun had risen high in the sky, and its rays streamed into the room. She thought of the hill she was going to climb on her way back. Well, what was it compared to what she had resolved? When Tifang waved her farewell, she moved on with light, bouncy steps.

The elders sat in a semicircle in tawh hall. Muyang sat on a stool close to Tita. The boy's mother sat on the other side of him. Behind the semicircle, four other women sat waiting. After some moments, Akatcho came in, carrying a jug of wine. He poured it into the pot at the centre of the circle.

He then moved back and sat close to Nande, who was one of the three women present. Forkon rose and moved to the pot. He picked up the calabash and filled it. Then he moved to the door, sprinkled some of it on the threshold, and mumbled some words.

Tita was not following the ceremony. What his mother had told him the night before still pierced his mind. How could his father have engaged him to a girl without telling him? Nande was beautiful, no doubt. But she was engaged to Akatcho, for whom his admiration was growing daily.

Forkon's voice brought him back to the present. "We are asking our ancestors to bless and protect our young father and to give him many sons." He moved over to the young couple.

"Tita, do you want Muyang as your first wife?"

"Yes."

"Muyang, do you want Tita as your husband?"

She nodded shyly. Tita's mother made a sign to her.

"Yes," she said, biting her nails.

Forkon called Fomujang to his side. He drank from his cup and handed it to the other. Fomujang drank and in turn handed it to Tita. The young man drank half its content and passed it over to Muyang, who emptied it. Forkon took the cup from the girl's hands.

As he resumed his seat, Forkon looked at Akatcho. "Come and serve your fathers."

The young man jumped up, filled the calabash, and began filling the horns of the men. There was a buzz of conversation as the men talked among themselves. After some time, Forkon raised his voice. "My children, we are through with you. If you feel like going outside, you are quite free to do so."

Tita had begun to rise when his mother laid a restraining hand on his knee. She winked at Tifang, who had been watching the ceremony in silence. He had told the men that he was in Ngwokwong to take Nande back to Zang, to help her mother. That was reasonable enough, and nobody imagined that there was something else on his mind.

He coughed significantly to attract attention. Slowly he stood up and joined his palms before him.

"My brothers and sisters of Ngwokwong, it is wonderful how the gods and our ancestors do things. I told you earlier that I am here to take Nande back to Zang. Well, it is a wonder to me that she still bears my name and still stays under my roof." He paused as the others exchanged looks.

"Something has been eating me up, and not able to bear it any longer, I thought it wise to come to you. Incidentally and luckily, I must say, *all* of you." He threw a sideways glance at Fomujang.

"A few days ago, Fomujang carried the traditional jug of wine to me, asking my daughter's hand in marriage to his son. I accepted. Little did I know that what seemed to have passed and been forgotten was going to stir up the flame again."

Fomujang's brows gathered. He was getting Tifang straight. His cheekbones stood out beneath the skin. He raised his eyes and gave the other a look that could have lit a house on fire. Tifang's breathing became short, irregular gasps that threatened to choke him. He thought for a split second to tell the people to forget what he had been saying. But that force that snatches away a man's will power, leaving him the helpless victim of the forces of evil, invaded him.

All in the room stared at him in discomfort. He forced himself to go on.

"A few months back, our departed father visited me with the traditional jug, asking my daughter's hand in marriage to his son. The young man's repeated absences brought a stop to further negotiations. Two days ago, Tita's mother came to me and made me to understand that Tita was urging her to carry on where his father had stopped. I was quite confused with the developments. That is why I am here, so that a solution may be found to this problem."

Tifang ended his short speech and sat down. He avoided looking in Fomujang's direction. The latter was fuming, but he managed to keep himself under control. Akatcho was dazed. What he just heard meant that Nande would not be his. How could this be possible? He threw a desperate glance at her. The girl had buried her face in her palms and rested her chin on the lap of the woman beside her. She was sobbing noiselessly.

Tita was staring at the floor. He could not stand up and tell the people that it was his last intention to want to seize Nande from Akatcho. He could not tell them that his late father had never discussed marriage with him. He reflected that that would bring much humiliation to his mother. He believed within him that whatever his mother was after, it was out of her love for him. But she definitely was not taking the right path, he told himself. He felt helpless, as anger and uncertainty gripped him. Muyang was looking at him in disbelief. So he had been lying to her. She succumbed to the anger and shame building up in her, and her tears began to flow freely.

It took Forkon quite a while to digest the recent revelations. When he began to speak, those sitting close to him could hear the gnashing of his teeth. "We must admit", he began, "that the situation is a complex one." Now that our father has gone on a very long journey, how do we know for certain what his intentions were? Not that I doubt the declaration of our dear brother Tifang." He paused to choose his words. "Our fathers of long ago had the wisdom to request the presence of a witness during occasions like the one in question. May we ask Tifang who accompanied our father then?"

There was a moment of uneasy silence as Tifang thought of what to say. Tita's mother had overlooked that point. He looked in her direction helplessly. She could only stare back, her eyes pleading for him to find a name.

"He came along with Tebug," Tifang managed to say. Tebug was the younger brother of Tita's mother. He was not there to speak for himself. There would be ample time to get him into the arrangement before he would ever be contacted.

Forkon and Abanda exchanged looks. They sensed that something was not quite straight. After they consulted for a moment, Forkon turned towards Fomujang.

"Who was your witness when you visited our brother from Zang to ask for his daughter's hand?"

Fomujang sighed deeply and replied, "Gyam and Awah were there."

Forkon exchanged a few words with Abanda again, while a wave of uneasy conversation swept across the room. At that instant, Akatcho slipped noiselessly out of the hut. Tita saw him leave and sneaked out after him.

Forkon straightened on his stool and waved for silence to return. "I believe we have all been wondering what attitude to adopt with this new development. I have just consulted with Abanda, and it seems to us that the best way forward is to confide in the wisdom of our ancestors. Our father is not here to confirm what our brother Tifang has just revealed. We need to call on our ancestors and put this case into their hands. A wrestling bout shall be organised between our two sons. Let our two young men stand."

All heads turned left and right, wondering where they had disappeared to. Abanda jumped to his feet. "I fear they may hurt themselves. We must stop them before it is too late." He rushed out, followed by the others.

"Do you hear me? Wait for me, please! I have something to tell you," Tita shouted desperately. Akatcho moved on. The other's voice only angered him the more. He quickened his steps. What could that traitor want to talk to him about other than false words of consolation? He was sure that Muyang must have talked to Tita about his impending marriage to Nande.

Tita ran and caught up with him. He laid a warm hand on his friend's shoulder. The wrong side of Akatcho had been provoked. Those who knew him well would have let him alone for some time until his anger subsided. Tita had only seen the calm and reserved side of Akatcho.

"Please, you must listen to me." Tita tried to hold Akatcho to a standstill. The latter was all the more infuriated. His body shook like one in the pitiless grip of malaria. His breath came in quick, short gasps. He pushed Tita violently away from him. Tita's pride, too, was stabbed. He steadied himself and stood firmly in Akatcho's way. Another attempt at pushing him out of the way met with firm resistance.

"Calm yourself, and let's talk. You should not go on behaving like a wild beast." Tita was running out of patience.

Akatcho could stand the sight of the other no more. He kicked out wildly, and his leg caught the other in the ribs. Tita winced in pain and bent double, holding his side. Akatcho made to move on, but like an enraged gorilla, the other pounced on him and seized him around the middle in a powerful grip. Tita planted his feet firmly on the ground and pushed the other brutally. Akatcho felt his body thrown backwards. His right heel hit a stone, and he lost his balance. He fell backwards, Tita above him. As he neared the ground, he freed his right hand and tried to catch himself. His right elbow hit the ground with a force that gave him a nasty jar. At the same time, his left leg shot upwards, throwing the other off balance. Tita fell flat on his back. Just then Akatcho groaned with pain and spread-eagled on the ground.

"The gods have spoken," a clear voice rang out. The boys looked up and saw the people they had left in the hall moving towards them. Abanda came up to Akatcho and went down on one knee. He looked at the boy's right arm.

"His arm is bleeding. It needs immediate attention."

Forkon came up. Tita was on his feet and looking down worriedly at his friend.

"He has to be taken immediately to Bawuru," Forkon said. Bawuru was the renowned medicine man from Tonokwo.

As the other elders joined Abanda to help the young men back to their feet, Forkon caressed his white beard slowly, as his mind flew back to the time when he had been about the same age as the young men. He saw himself and Ndaneng furiously engaged in a fight on the shore of Aghah, close to the spot where Enjoh usually came to fetch water. It was only the arrival of the young woman on the scene that had put an end to the struggle. Enjoh had been the village beauty, and most young men at the time had rivalled to catch her attention. Two young men had attracted her, and she was not sure which of the two she fancied more. Forkon was a few moons younger than Ndaneng. The former had approached his father, and the traditional wine had been carried to Enjoh's father. Ndaneng had realised that Enjoh's heart was tilting towards Forkon.

Then Forkon's father had been taken ill, and he, the only son, had accompanied him to the great medicine man of Etwii. It had taken a full moon for his father to regain his health. They had hardly returned to their compound in Ngwokwong when Forkon had rushed off to visit Enjoh. They had embraced each other warmly and had shared stories of the past days when they had had to be apart. Something had changed in the young woman, and Forkon had sensed it, but in the excitement of the moment did not think much about it. He had been away for many days, and she might have felt abandoned and become very upset about it. In the weeks ahead, Forkon had promised himself, he was going to crowd her and fill her with so much love that she would quickly forget the stress she must have gone through.

But as the days had passed by, Forkon had quickly realised that the more attempts he made to gain Enjoh's full attention the more distant she became. Then it had become obvious that she was pregnant.

"I will go with Akatcho to Tonokwo," Tita spoke, looking at Forkon for approval.

Forkon did not move. The young man edged closer, saying, "I want to stay with him until his elbow is healed. May I?" Tita raised his voice, uncertain whether Forkon had heard him the first time but had not wanted to react.

The old man started and shook his head to dispel the unwanted thoughts of the past. "What did you say, my son?"

Tita repeated his question.

The older man was pleased with Tita's words. "You can visit him whenever you have the chance." He placed his right hand on the young man's shoulder and waited for the others to move out of hearing distance. "It is about time you went up to the kob for the one-week traditional stay among the ancestors of the land." As they walked towards tawh, Abanda left the others and joined Tita and Forkon.

Tita showed no surprise about this custom of the land. Abanda had briefed him earlier. "Who will bring me food and water?" he asked.

"You must choose among your friends the one you trust most," Abanda replied and signalled them to join the others. He and Forkon started walking, but Tita stood his ground.

"Akatcho is the one I trust most, and I want to tell him so – and now."

The determination showed in the young man's face. Abanda walked off quickly and returned with Akatcho. A cloth had been tied around the latter's right elbow to stop the bleeding. The pain had subsided, but he was not ready for any long explanations before these two elders of the land. He was sick at the thought of Nande becoming Tita's wife. A thousand thoughts had gone through his mind since the elders had arrived to put an end to their fight. One thing was clear to him. No one would take Nande away from him. He was still wondering how he would ensure that as they approached Forkon and Tita.

"I am sorry to have caused you harm, Akatcho. I will never attempt to take Nande from you. I was never part of whatever happened."

Akatcho was not sure he had heard right. He searched the faces of the two elders, and they nodded in support of Tita's words.

He did not know what to say. So he just nodded to show that he understood. Tita edged closer and held Akatcho in a warm embrace.

"You are the one I trust the most, and I will need you." Tita stared into Akatcho's eyes, and the other stared back, smiling his approval and mutual love.

"Will you run and join the others, before they start wondering what is happening here?" Forkon urged, and Abanda left with the two boys. Forkon looked at them as they walked away, but his mind again wandered into the past.

Enjoh had given birth to Ba-yoh. The birth had been a difficult one, and she had not survived. Forkon had grieved for many moons. He had been certain Ba-yoh was not his son. The boy had been the exact replica of Ndaneng. When Ba-yoh turned five years, Ndaneng's father, then fon of Ngwokwong, had gone on the long journey to seek the ancestors of the land. He had returned two months later as his son Ndaneng. And the name Ndaneng had quickly disappeared from everyday use, to be replaced by "the fon" or "the father of Ngwokwong". Forkon recollected how he had carried Ndaneng's meals up the Kob Azah for a full week. Full of guilt for the harm he had caused Forkon, the new fon-to-be then had asked for forgiveness, and at the summit of the kob, the two had forged a bond that had stood the test of time. Forkon had put the past behind him, and both men had grown very fond of each other. Ba-yoh had inherited nothing from his father other than being his physical replica. As a young man, he had showed neither the physical prowess of his generation nor the shrewdness expected of a future leader of his people. What if the man had survived his father and were today being prepared to rule Ngwokwong? The future of Ngwokwong would be very bleak.

"Would you have prevented it had destiny not decided otherwise?" The question had dropped unto Forkon's mind as if someone had voiced it next to him.

The old man shivered violently and came back to the present. The others had disappeared in the distance.

"I would not want Ba-yoh to succeed me. He is not the leader I see for Ngwokwong when the time comes for me to join our ancestors" the fon had confided in Forkon as they shared a calabash of *Raffia* wine one day. They had been watching the young man, then fifteen years old, as he had shied away from a wrestling exercise that all his mates had been involved in.

Forkon made a few steps to try and catch up with the others, when a sudden thought seemed to strike him, and he stopped abruptly, his mouth slowly opening and his eyes widening but focussing on nothing around him.

"Could Ndaneng have decided to take Ba-yoh away with him, as he had seen no future for Ngwokwong with the latter at its helm? Had he returned immediately as a spirit to fulfil Djalo's curse?" Forkon had voiced the question unintentionally, and he turned his head around, hoping no one had heard him.

He shook his head and tried to clear his mind. This was for the gods to decipher. He walked quickly away from the spot and refused to let his mind to wander into the past again.

The two young people sat close together on the flat stone, deep in conversation.

"This is where I usually sat when I thought of you."

Akatcho gently pulled Nande's hand towards him.

"Do not exert force on your arm. You remember what Bawuru said, I hope?" she warned.

"Yes. He said I must not touch anything hard with my arm for at least ten days. But I know that your hand is softer than the marrow in a chicken's limb."

"Oh! Do not exaggerate. I do not want you to stay away from me again. The two moons you spent in Tonokwo were a period of hell for me."

The young man wrapped her with his left arm.

"What do you think of the hut Father has built for you?" she asked, looking at the newly built hut behind Fomujang's compound.

"Father has done a great job. We are celebrating our marriage tomorrow. How do you feel?"

"Like a chick under its mother's feathers," she said, laughing.

"Do you know something?" he asked, smiling broadly. "I have seen the calabash of palm oil which mother has prepared for you."

She slapped him lightly on the back.

"You will see. When the oil is rubbed on me, you will be the first I will catch. If I do not smear that nice face of yours with palm oil tomorrow, then my name is not Nande."

He smiled and stood up.

"Let's go into the house now and see what those old people are doing."

They walked towards the house. Fomujang came out and blew his nose noisily, directing the waste from his nostrils onto a plant with greenish-yellowish leaves.

"What a period we have gone through, my children." He smiled at the young couple. Akatcho was admiring the leaves of the sisal plant.

"Father, have you noticed these plants you are desecrating?" He pointed at the multicoloured leaves.

Fomujang looked more closely at the sisal plant.

"So, those are the plants about which great things were prophesied by the stranger to the fon. So occupied have we been these past months that I have not paid the least attention to them."

"What stranger, Father?" Akatcho asked.

"What market day is tomorrow?"

"Tang," Gyam answered, joining the others. "What is the idea?"

"The day after tomorrow is Tad market day. You two will accompany me to the big market, and with luck we may find the stranger. He will tell us what to do next with these plants." And, talking as if to himself, Fomujang added, "Could the secret of this plant have prevented the death of Djalo, his cows, and Ba-yoh? How can these plants stop raging wildfire? How can they be an instrument of peace?"

"What stranger? What are you talking about?"

Fomujang pointed at the leaves. Gyam stared at the plant.

"Certainly this is a period of surprises. So these plants are beginning to produce coloured leaves with sharp edges. The gods alone know what these plants are."

He turned to the young people. "Come, my children. I am not waiting for tomorrow to start drinking the wine marking your union."

"Tita will attend my marriage?" Akatcho asked hopefully.

"Certainly. In four days' time, the Fon of Ngwokwong will return. All the time you were away treating your arm, he kept repeating that you must be his right-hand man. The ancestors are preparing him for his new role up the kob. He has been up there for the past two days. He resisted going up there, insisting that you must return first, as you are to be the only one to visit him during his week of initiation. But our tradition had to be respected, and we could not wait any longer. He really likes you. Indeed, he felt happier to go up to the kob if only I, your father, would take his food to him. It has not been easy for me going up this steep hill these past two days. But that viper of his mother is slowly wearing away with shame. Ha! She thought she could snatch away my daughter from me."

Nande smiled. She asked, "Did she plan the confusion?"

"And she failed. Let's forget about that." Gyam beamed at them.

At least her father had not planned it. Nande sighed with relief.

Gyam caught them by their hands and marched them after Fomujang into the hut. "This has been a period in time," Gyam murmured to himself.

"Father," Akatcho spoke, pulling a stool for Nande to sit on, "I would like to replace you and take Tita's food up to him for his remaining days up the kob, if you will allow me."

"That is what Tita wants, to see you stand by him, as Forkon had stood by his father." The older man pulled a jug from the side of the bamboo bed, and Akatcho rose to serve. Gyam's horn was already out and waiting.

"Tita will be pleasantly surprised to see the younger version of Fomujang visiting him today. You will need to get ready to go to tawh and take the food along."

After drinking from his horn, Fomujang stretched out his arm, and Nande accepted the horn from her father-in-law to be.

"In a few days we will celebrate the union of the most beautiful couple in Ngwokwong." The man gave one of his rare smiles.

The room darkened as Tengu approached. She lowered the bucket of water from her head and stepped into the hut.

"I cannot wait to carry my grandchildren in my arms." She wrapped her arms around Nande, who had risen from her stool to help the older woman.

Gyam rose from his stool and raised the almost-empty calabash. "Please sit, Akatcho's mother." The man looked so serious that Nande was a bit frightened.

"Akatcho, where is your horn?"

"The calabash is empty," Akatcho said, smiling. He knew what Gyam was after. He stretched out his horn all the same, and Gyam emptied the thick dregs into it.

As one who is performing a very important ceremony, Gyam nodded to the young man. "If your mother's wish is to come true, then you must drink all of that."

Akatcho sipped from his horn, and his mouth twisted with disgust, but he swallowed. Then the two young people burst out laughing and rushed out of the room.

Fomujang shifted his stool to make way for Tengu. "Your son will replace me today and for the rest of the days to take up food to Tita". And speaking to no one in particular, he whispered, "In another five days, Fon Azah of Ngwokwong will be back again among his people."

Fon Tangum

Fon Tangum was born in Ngwokwong at the dawn of independence in Cameroon. He grew up in the hills and valleys of Gam and is very conversant with the traditions and beliefs of the people of this remarkable land.

He attended the Hassan II University and graduated with an Ingénieur d'Application en Génie Rural certificate. Much later he enrolled in the University of Southampton in England, where he obtained an MSc in Engineering for Development.

He works for international organisations involved in the fight against poverty across most of Africa. He believes, and likes to share with whoever will listen, that poor communities will become poverty-free when their autonomy and self-reliance are built around the locally available resources, knowledge and culture.

His first novel, *IFUH*, was published in Cameroon in 2007.

He is married to Laetitia Nande, and they have three children: Tameri, Afor, and Bessem.

Lightning Source UK Ltd.
Milton Keynes UK
UKHW010126140722
405812UK00001B/9